"If you don't feel like answering the question, I'll be happy to squash you all like bugs."

"Gravity!"

Latticenail

"For the first time in pageant history, we have a tie for first place!"

As the announcer called out their names and the audience cheered, Amelia and Latticenail joined hands and headed back out to the stage.

✦ Amelia Rosequartz

"*Not to toot my own horn or anything, but I know a lotta boys who'd kill for a chance with me!*"

My Status *as an* Assassin *Obviously* Exceeds *the* Hero's

NOVEL

3

WRITTEN BY
**Matsuri
Akai**

ILLUSTRATED BY
Tozai

Airship

Seven Seas Entertainment

CONTENTS

ANSATSUSHA DE ARU ORE NO SUTETASU GA YUUSHA
YORI MO AKIRAKA NI TSUYOI NODAGA VOL. 3
© 2019 Matsuri Akai
Illustrated by Tozai
First published in Japan in 2019 by OVERLAP Inc., Ltd., Tokyo.
English translation rights arranged with OVERLAP Inc., Ltd., Tokyo.

Seven Seas press and purchase enquiries can be sent to
Marketing Manager Lianne Sentar at press@gomanga.com.
Information regarding the distribution and purchase of
digital editions is available from Digital Manager CK Russell
at digital@gomanga.com.

Follow Seven Seas Entertainment online at
sevenseasentertainment.com.

TRANSLATION: Colby W.
ADAPTATION: Leigh Teetzel
COVER DESIGN: Hanase Qi
INTERIOR LAYOUT & DESIGN: Clay Gardner
COPY EDITOR: Meg van Huygen
PROOFREADER: Brian Kearney
LIGHT NOVEL EDITOR: T. Anne
PRINT MANAGER: Rhiannon Rasmussen-Silverstein
PRODUCTION MANAGER: Lissa Pattillo
MANAGING EDITOR: Julie Davis
ASSOCIATE PUBLISHER: Adam Arnold
PUBLISHER: Jason DeAngelis

ISBN: 978-1-64827-660-6
Printed in Canada
First Printing: January 2022
10 9 8 7 6 5 4 3 2 1

CHAPTER 1

The Ring

POV: AMELIA ROSEQUARTZ

As soon as Akira stepped out of the building, the whole house went eerily quiet. I noticed the hero stealing glances at me from time to time, but he didn't say a word. Asahina, the boy who'd taken Night to task a moment ago, seemed pensive and lost in thought. Eventually, the boy named Nanase dared to speak up, albeit with a heavy dose of hesitation in his voice.

"S-so, uh... What brings you to the beastfolk domain, Your Highness? And where exactly were you guys planning on going from here?" he asked, then looked away the moment I tried to make eye contact with him.

I let out a heavy sigh. "Well, our ultimate destination is still the Demon Lord's castle in the heart of Volcano. We only came to Brute because we needed Crow's help to fix Akira's sword. I'm not sure if we're going to head straight for the Demon Lord after this or not, though. Still need to talk with Akira and Night about that."

I deliberately chose to ignore their request to accompany us, since it sounded like Akira was pretty opposed to the idea.

"Now, can I ask you all something?" I added. Nanase nodded, so I scanned the group and addressed the five members of the hero's party who were not seated in chairs. "What about the rest of you? You disagree with these two, am I right? You'd rather not join up with Akira?"

The Ueno girl with the funny accent and the boy named Waki (who I assumed was an animal trainer, given that he was surrounded by tiny animals) nodded in confirmation. The other three, however, didn't seem so sure.

"Well, if you want any hope of convincing us to let you tag along, you'll need to come to an agreement among yourselves first. Luckily for you, Akira and Night are still pretty exhausted, so you'll have plenty of time to do that while they recover," I said, and the hero (who'd clearly been at quite a loss) bowed his head to me politely.

"We'll do just that. Thank you for your consideration," he said, before rising from his seat.

Asahina, who was sitting next to him, also stood up, gave a little bow, then followed the hero into the next room, and the other party members followed suit. They were all very polite, and it was obvious they came from a society very different from our own—though I'd heard it said that the eastern nation of Yamato on the human continent had a similar culture of respect. The hero who founded that country must have also been from that "Japan" place where Akira grew up.

"What do you think, Night? Would Akira be happy to have them along?" I asked, now that he and I were the only two remaining in the room.

The little feline looked up at me with piercing golden eyes from his perch atop the table. Then, after mulling it over a bit, he shrugged his shoulders. *"Hard to say. Even though I'm telepathically connected to him, it's hard to tell what's going through that boy's head. I do know Master was apparently rather close with that impertinent little rat,"* said Night, referring to the Asahina boy he'd had a bit of a scuffle with. He was probably feeling a little annoyed that there was now someone here who probably knew Akira far better than he did. *"Also, that animal trainer boy and the girl with the strange accent are clearly not fond of Master, to put it lightly. Hard to see any way that having them along would be beneficial."*

I nodded in agreement, though I didn't have much room to judge whether other people would get in Akira's way, given that I had nearly murdered him down in the labyrinth. I hadn't wanted to, of course, and if I had only been stronger, that demon wouldn't have been able to take control of me. Thankfully, Akira's Shadow Magic was able to heal his wounds completely, otherwise he would have most certainly died down there.

Night, having picked up on my sudden glumness, peered into my eyes with concern.

"You can't let what happened down in the labyrinth get to you, Lady Amelia. In the end, Master survived, and that's all that matters. You didn't hurt him; Mahiro did. I promise you Master

doesn't blame you for what happened," Night said, trying to reassure me.

"Yeah. You're right. Thanks, Night," I said, forcing a smile.

Night nodded, buying my response, then fell back into deep thought, so I left him there on the table and exited the building. I found my way to a forest on the outskirts of town, where it almost felt like the trees were welcoming me as a member of the high elf nobility. We elves had always lived in harmony with the forest, after all. Long ago, we grew tired of the wars of men who were seeking wealth and dominion, and we instead became the stalwart guardians of the Sacred Forest, fearing that the other races might cut down the Holy Tree were they to get their hands on it. And the Holy Tree was not to be disturbed under any circumstances.

Gah, why am I thinking about this now?

Throughout my entire life, I'd retreated into the forest and asked the trees for their counsel whenever I was faced with a difficult decision or my thoughts reached an impasse. I pressed my forehead up against the bark of one, yet all I could think of was the moment my hand plunged through Akira's abdomen.

"You don't understand, Night," I whispered, my clenched fists trembling. "While it's true that I would never have hurt Akira like that of my own volition, I...I have to admit, the thought of leaving scars on Akira's body that would forever remind him of me was...exhilarating, in a way."

After all, there was no doubt in my mind that if he found a way to return to his world, he'd take it in an instant and leave me behind. He'd told me how his mother was very ill, and he couldn't expect his little sister to pick up his slack forever. Perhaps what I feared most was him one day forgetting about me after he left. Maybe he would find some other girl who was prettier than me and more fit to stand by his side, and maybe they would get married and have a happy family together. But if I left an actual, tangible mark on his body, then maybe he would still remember me even after he grew old and senile. Which I knew was a rather disgusting thing to say—no one should ever *want* to harm their beloved—yet there was part of me that felt weirdly happy to have wounded him like that.

What a weak and spiteful woman I was, jealous of a hypothetical woman I'd never even met. How pathetic. As I was lost in self-loathing, I heard the sound of a branch snap somewhere above me. I looked up and saw jet-black eyes piercing through the veil of night straight into mine. They crinkled in amusement.

"So *that's* what's been bothering you, huh? Heh. And here I thought it might actually be something serious."

My mouth went dry, and my mind went blank. Eventually, I managed to force out a single word through my dumbfounded stupor—the name of the person to whom those eyes belonged.

"A-Akira..."

POV: ODA AKIRA

I LEAPT DOWN from the tree to stand in front of a very startled Amelia, whose shoulders were trembling.

"A-Akira... How much of that did you hear?" she asked.

"Oh, I don't know... All of it? I was hanging out up there before you even got here," I admitted, scratching the back of my neck sheepishly.

Her face went deathly pale.

It really was just a coincidence, though. After hearing Crow's answer to my question back in his workshop, I'd headed for the nearby forest to do some serious thinking. Being up high in a tree had always been the best place for contemplation, and while I genuinely wasn't trying to eavesdrop, the truth of the matter was that I was just too lost in thought to notice her arrival until it was too late. Though I had a feeling that explanation would do little to alleviate her current embarrassment. Her naturally pale face was now white as a sheet. I placed a hand on her head, hoping it might calm her down a bit.

"Don't worry so much. I'm not just gonna up and abandon you one day, and I could never forget you, even if I wanted to," I said.

Sure, I cared a lot about my mom and my sister, Yui, but I cared about Amelia just as much. I could see tears welling up in her eyes as she clutched my black cloak with all her might.

"You mean it? You really won't abandon or forget me?" she asked, pleading. There was a puppy-dog look in her eyes making it hard to not squeeze her tight.

"Yeah, I promise." I nodded. "Besides, if anything, *you're* the one who's out of *my* league. Just in terms of looks, even someone like the hero would be a better match for you, as much as I hate to admit it."

Amelia scrunched up her face as I drew one of my black daggers, forged from the remains of the Yato-no-Kami, and placed it into her hand.

"No way. I don't like that guy at all. You're way stronger and cooler than he is, and... Wait. What are you doing?" she asked, and I smirked.

It was true that the hero was far weaker than me, but less cool? Not by any traditional definition of the word, anyway. There was no way Amelia and I would have ended up together if I hadn't been her savior and lone companion through a very specific crisis. It was like the suspension bridge effect, in a way. She needed a hero, and I was there.

With the dagger now firmly in Amelia's grasp, I held her hand in my right hand and brought the knife up to my left. Amelia recoiled a bit, confused.

"I dunno how you do things in this world, but back home, we have a custom where a man and woman who've sworn to spend the rest of their lives with each other exchange rings worn on the fourth fingers of their left hands. We call it the 'ring finger' for that very reason. It's not something I ever saw myself doing, so I don't know the specific rules or history behind engagement rings and wedding rings, but when two people each have rings around their fingers like that, it's a symbol of their bond." I did my best to explain as I traced the tip of the dagger in her hand around the third joint of my ring finger. Even through the darkness, I could see blood trickling out, running down my arm before dripping onto the ground. No ordinary blade could cut through my skin in this world, but the Yato-no-Kami was no ordinary blade.

"Wh-what are you doing?" Amelia asked, her eyes wide as she watched me dig the dagger deep enough to leave a scar, but not so deep as to hit anything vital.

"How's that? Looks at least a little bit like a ring, doesn't it?" I asked, holding my hand up to the moonlight to see the bright-red ring just above my knuckle. "You said you wanted to leave your mark on me, didn't you? Well, now you have."

Amelia looked back and forth between the dagger in her hand and my finger. "A ring...as a symbol of the bond between a man and a woman..." she murmured, trying to wrap her head around the idea. Then, she placed the dagger back in my hand and, without even a second thought, began guiding it around her own slender ring finger. "I feel bad for causing you more pain, but at the same time...it feels so good to share something so precious with you."

Standing next to me, she held her own hand up to inspect it. Seeing Amelia bleeding normally would have made me sick to my stomach, yet for whatever reason, it felt oddly comforting tonight. Suddenly, Crow's heart-wrenching voice rang through my ears.

"The thing that terrifies me more than anything else in the world...is when I try to reach out for something and my fingers touch nothing."

Perhaps I wouldn't always be able to reach out and grab hold of Amelia whenever I wanted to. Given how powerful the demons were, there was a very real chance she and I could have both died down there if Crow hadn't shown up when he did.

But so long as we both had these scars around our fingers, she and I would be bound for eternity.

"Amelia, I'd break every bone in my body for you, if that's what you wanted. I'll happily wear any scars you see fit to adorn me with. But in exchange, I want you to tell me everything. Anytime you want me to do something, or anytime something's bothering you, you come and tell me. I'll do whatever's in my power to make things right."

I knelt down and planted a kiss on the back of her left hand. Then, realizing I was probably making a giant fool of myself, I looked up to see her cheeks flushed bright red, before she placed her hands on my cheeks.

"All right. Then I want you to promise me something too. Promise you'll never forget me, never go anywhere without me, never die and leave me behind, and never, ever look at anyone else but me."

I stood up and wrapped Amelia in my arms; her tiny frame fit perfectly. "Your wish is my command, my dear. And I'll do whatever I can to grant it."

The "never go anywhere without me" part was probably a bit unrealistic, but I felt confident I could safely commit to the rest. I certainly had no intention of dying on her, or forgetting her, or being unfaithful to her.

Cradled in my arms, Amelia smiled, truly content. It was the first time I'd seen her smile like she meant it since the incident down in the labyrinth. It was the sort of smile she only used when she was alone with me and Night—not the fake one she gave to outsiders just to be polite.

I still wanted to go home to Japan, my mom, and my sister someday. But right here, in this moment, there was nothing I wanted more than to hold on tight to that smile.

POV: ASAHINA KYOUSUKE

THE ROOM CROW had so kindly let us borrow was the largest in the house, and the seven of us were all currently spread out across it, trying to relax. I stood near the door with my back against the wall and my arms folded.

Princess Amelia had instructed us to come to an agreement as a group on what we wanted to do going forward, yet no one was saying a word. Usually, it was Satou who tried to lead discussions, but he hadn't said a word since we left the other room. Even Waki and Ueno, the two members who could generally be counted on to kick up a fuss, were silent. Nanase and Tsuda both looked awfully restless, while Hosoyama seemed cool as ever.

I closed my eyes and tried to go over the whole situation in my head. It was safe to assume that Akira's ultimate objective was the same as ours: to return to Japan. If anything, he probably felt more anxious to make it home than the rest of us, as he had to take care of his mother and sister. So why was he moving separately? Perhaps it was simply that he had a different idea about the best way to achieve that goal, but as I understood it, the only way to return home after being summoned to another world was to slay the final boss—though I was by no means an expert on the genre, having only heard bits and pieces secondhand about the novels Akira loved to read.

Hang on. Could it be...?

My eyes shot wide open, and Tsuda, who'd been standing directly across from me, jumped in shock. I turned my eyes to look at Satou, who was staring pensively at the floor. "Tell me something, Satou... Do you have any intention of trying to slay the Demon Lord?"

Everyone looked at me as I broke the silence, then over to Satou in anticipation of his response. The boy scrunched up his handsome face like he was pouting and shook his head. This was a grave sign indeed.

If there was one thing the knights back in Retice drilled into our heads each day during training, it was that the Demon Lord could be slain only by the hero with the sacred blade and the Holy Sword Extra Skill, and right now, that hero was Satou. As long as we met those requirements, defeating him would be a piece of cake. Our job as the hero's companions was to see him safely to the Demon Lord's lair, but if the hero had no will or desire to slay the Demon Lord, then there was nothing anyone could do.

"Sorry, guys, but I really don't see a need to go and slay the Demon Lord right now," Satou said.

In fairness, he had a point. The Demon Lord had yet to show himself in any recognizable way since we'd been summoned from Earth, and only Akira's team claimed to have seen demons first-hand. We couldn't completely rule out the possibility that the incident with the monsters flooding out of the labyrinth in Ur was nothing more than an accident. My Intuition skill begged to differ, but that didn't count as hard evidence.

"Th-then how are we supposed to make it back home to Japan, huh?!" cried Waki.

This was perhaps the primary counterargument. Up until then, we'd all believed slaying the Demon Lord was our one and only ticket back home, and it was what we'd been working toward ever since our arrival.

"Whaddya mean, ya don't see a need? Weren't you the one who got us all gussied up to go and take 'im out in the first place?" Ueno asked.

She was right. Satou *was* the one who'd made a rousing speech to that effect. But that was back when we all still believed the royal family of Retice had our best interests in mind. They told us the Demon Lord was committing acts of tyranny and terror all across this world, and that we were the only ones with the power to stop him.

"Look, I don't have all the answers, okay?" Satou responded. "All I know is the one who told us the Demon Lord's the root of all evil was the same guy who used his daughter to place curses on all of us. And from what I've seen, none of the people in any of the towns we've been to since seem like they're oppressed or under threat from any demons at the moment."

Ueno and Waki looked at each other, their eyes wide, as they realized the truth of what was being said. It was true; the places we'd seen were all bustling with life and prosperity. Even in the eastern nation of Yamato, which was the closest point on the continent to the demons' domain, none of the citizenry seemed even slightly fazed by the supposed threat of a demon invasion. Nanase and Tsuda simply looked pensive, perhaps fearing the worst for the classmates we'd left back at the castle in Retice.

"Um, are we all forgetting that Oda literally *just* got seriously injured by the demons?" asked Hosoyama, raising her hand. "Do we think he's lying about that, or does that not constitute a serious threat?"

I squinted, feeling skeptical. Her words were clearly those of someone who felt we should take Akira's side on this issue, yet I couldn't tell whether she had come to that conclusion independently or was merely giving her classmate the benefit of the doubt. I always had a hard time reading her; she wasn't easy to read like Waki or Ueno.

"Yeah, and you know what else? Akira's stronger than I am," Satou jumped in. "Probably has been since we were summoned to this world, now that I think about it. Even with all our powers combined, we probably couldn't hold a candle to him. So if he's right, and these demons really are so evil and terrifying that even *he* barely survived one encounter with them, then the rest of us don't have a chance in hell against them, let alone the Demon Lord. As it stands now, we're barely stronger than the average warrior in this world."

That was the first time I'd ever heard Satou admit something like that. He was always so self-assured and seemed to despise showing any signs of weakness or vulnerability. Nanase, too, looked like he could hardly believe the words coming out of the hero's mouth.

"Look, I wanna go home just as badly as you guys do," Satou continued, "and I promise you Akira does too. But he doesn't seem to think slaying the Demon Lord is an urgent priority right now. Have you considered that maybe it's because he knows none of us stand a chance of winning?"

A wise deduction, perhaps. Were this a video game or a fantasy novel, the heroes would likely make a valiant stand against the Demon Lord, be promptly overwhelmed by his power, then spend a long time building up their strength so they could defeat him the next time. But this was real life, unfortunately, and in real life there were no extra lives or convenient plot devices. If we faced the Demon Lord now, he would slaughter us all without mercy.

"I can tell you guys with 100 percent confidence that Akira is probably more determined than any of us to make it home to Japan, and he probably also knows better than any of us exactly what it's gonna take to accomplish that. Which is why I suggested we tag along with him to provide support," Satou finished, and everyone nodded to show their understanding.

"Gotcha. Was that your reasoning too, Kyousuke?" asked Nanase, turning toward me, the only other person on board with the idea initially.

"No, nothing like that. I simply wanted to support him however I could, as a friend. Though I admit I'd only drag him down at my current level," I replied. By now, Akira had grown far stronger than I could have imagined. If we traveled together, it would always be him protecting me, not the other way around. I was incapable of standing beside him on the battlefield. I hadn't witnessed his strength firsthand, mind you, but I could tell from a single glance the kinds of ordeals he'd been through.

"Well, I still don't trust 'im, for the record. I mean, it was his dang dagger in Saran's heart, for cryin' out loud! Maybe if he treated us like actual freakin' companions before that, I'd give 'im the benefit of the doubt, but no, he was always runnin' off doin' shady stuff all by his lonesome!" grumbled Ueno, crossing her arms and leaning against the wall.

"Didn't we already go over this? We all agreed Akira didn't kill the commander."

After our group left the castle, we held our first team strategy meeting in order to verify we were all free from the effects of the curse and set some ground rules. It was then that we all agreed—based on Akira's reaction to seeing Saran's blood-soaked corpse and the evil words that Satou allegedly overheard from the princess—that there was no way Akira could have killed him.

Ueno, clearly incensed, gripped at her hair in frustration. "I ain't sayin' he did! All I'm sayin' is that he's been actin' awful fishy ever since we got here, so we shouldn't just take his word as law!" she asserted.

I cocked my head, puzzled. Had she expected Akira's core personality to suddenly change because we'd been summoned to another world? He was always the loner looking at the rest of the class from afar, rolling his eyes as if we were all a bunch of fools and he was the only one who could see it. The only two classmates who ever attempted to interact with him were myself and Nanase.

"Yeah, I've gotta agree with Ueno here," said Waki. "If he wasn't wandering around behind our backs from the get-go, none of us would have suspected him in the first place. Well, other than Ryuusuke, maybe, but everyone knows those two have got beef."

The boy Waki was referring to was Oka Ryuusuke—one of his fellow soccer team members and our class's resident "life of the party." The tall, relatively handsome Oka had been going out of his way to taunt and badmouth Akira ever since the spring of our freshman year. I wasn't sure what the impetus for their antagonistic relationship was, but he was almost assuredly to blame for Akira having become even more reclusive in recent years. I asked Akira once if he'd ever said anything that might have offended Oka, and he didn't even know who I was referring to. This was fairly typical; he only reserved room in his brain for the things he cared about. I was sure he didn't remember Nanase's name either, despite them ostensibly being friends. Now that I thought about it, I remembered seeing Waki join in on Oka's Akira-bashing on a few occasions.

"I mean, yeah, we all know Akira's a lone wolf, to put it nicely." Nanase sighed. "Or, to put it not so nicely, he's a stubborn stick in the mud who's never willing to cooperate on any terms but his own. But that's just who he is."

I nodded in agreement, deciding to let Waki's comment go. Instead, I turned to Tsuda, who was hunched over in a corner, trying to be as invisible as possible.

"Any thoughts about all of this, Tsuda?" I asked.

He shot up, clearly shaken by my sudden address. This was the norm with him, and I had a hunch he didn't feel totally comfortable speaking with me. We were both members of the school's kendo team, but I was its captain. He probably felt like a bit of an outsider as well, having only taken up kendo in high school, and thus lacking the more chiseled body of a longtime member. His form was unassuming and almost feminine, and I could understand why he might be intimidated by me.

"Oh, um, w-well...I haven't really had many chances to interact with Oda myself, so I'm not a good judge of his character, but if you think he's trustworthy, Asahina, then I'm willing to have faith in him."

I couldn't help but blink. He was willing to trust Akira simply because I trusted him? That would imply that Tsuda respected me far more than I would have guessed. And here I thought the boy was terrified of me. *Just goes to show how bad I am at reading other people, I suppose.*

"What's your vote, Hosoyama? It's three against two now," I said, turning back to her. While Nanase hadn't given his vote yet, I was fairly certain he'd be on the pro-Akira side, which would make it four against two.

"If we want to join up with Oda, I'm totally fine with that," she said with an almost motherly smile. "Though we'd still need to get Princess Amelia's permission, which is another story entirely."

For whatever reason, that smile of hers gave me goosebumps. I couldn't suss out her intentions, and that made me anxious.

"Well, we don't even need to ask for Nanase's vote, then,

because we already have the majority," Satou concluded. "So, Waki and Ueno, what's it gonna be?"

We'd come this far as a team, but that didn't mean we had to stay together going forward. It had benefited us to stick together at first, since we had a common goal and were all equally unfamiliar with the world of Morrigan, but we were about to venture into far more dangerous territory, and it sounded like Satou was giving those who wanted it the chance to leave. Akira certainly wouldn't care who tagged along.

The two dissenters exchanged glances with one another, before letting out deep sighs of mutual resignation.

"Yeah, had a feeling that's what you guys would decide," said Waki.

"Well, I s'pose me not bein' Oda's biggest fan is my own personal problem. If that's what y'all have decided, I'll go with the flow," Ueno said.

This was good news. While they were both free to do as they pleased, losing them would have greatly upset our party's balance and fighting style. I wasn't especially worried; it wasn't as though they had anywhere else to go. Satou, however, breathed a sigh of relief.

"Cool, then it sounds like we just need to convince the princess now," said Nanase.

I nodded. We didn't know the first thing about Princess Amelia, but chances were she'd be a much harder nut to crack than Waki and Ueno. She was the single greatest obstacle between us and our end goal.

"Well, I guess we probably have until they depart from the beastfolk domain to convince them, right? And it sounds like Akira and his familiar are both going to need plenty of time to recuperate from their run-in with the demons."

It wasn't as though we didn't have time to sort things out, but we couldn't afford to rest on our laurels either.

"Hey, speaking of R&R, I heard there's gonna be a big festival in Uruk pretty soon," Waki said, suddenly changing the subject. "Heard about it from some of the girls on the boat ride over here."

For a bit of context: the stray cats of this world were far less friendly and much more cautious than those back in Japan, but an animal trainer like Waki could befriend them immediately, at which point they turned into the most affectionate cats one could ever meet. It was for this reason that Waki (or more specifically, his cats) often enjoyed attention from the ladies of this world. A swarm of them had surrounded him for the duration of the boat ride from Kantinen to Brute, all looking for a chance to pet his cats.

"A festival, eh? That *would* make for a nice change of pace. Maybe we should see if they're interested in checking it out?" suggested Satou, and the two girls of the group immediately lit up. I fully expected Hosoyama to be all over the idea of a festival, but apparently Ueno was too.

"But what kinda festival *is* it, do ya reckon?" Ueno asked Waki.

"Dunno. All they said was that it's the perfect chance for young women to strut their stuff."

That almost makes it sound like a fashion show of some sort, I thought to myself.

"What the heck does that mean…?" muttered Nanase. "And do we even know what the average 'festival' in this world entails?"

It was a fair question, to be sure. While to us Japanese, the word *festival* conjured up images of yukatas and fireworks and food stands, in some other countries, they were more like parades.

"H-hey, um, now that you mention it, I think I heard some of the older guys at the Adventurer's Guild talking about that," Tsuda chimed in hesitantly.

Likely due to his rather feminine appearance, Tsuda was frequently approached by other adventurers whenever we visited the Guild…or more specifically, the retired old men who still hung out at the Guild would try to pamper him with attention and drinks, which would draw the attention of the younger adventurers as well, and…well, you get the idea. I wasn't quite sure how it happened or when it started, but I was fairly certain that if anything were to happen to Tsuda, every adventurer in Ur would rush to his aid.

"They told me there's an annual contest there to determine who the most beautiful man and woman are across all races, and that it's being held in Uruk this year," Tsuda continued.

Aha. So it's like something of a Miss Universe competition, then. I had to wonder if those sorts of things were an inevitability in every world, or if people summoned from ours had introduced the concept. At the very least, it seemed the desire to crown a champion in any field was a universal constant.

"And while they said there's both a guys' competition and a girls' one, the girls' one is by far the most popular. O-oh, and, uh…" Tsuda trailed off, his face turning suddenly pale.

"And what?" asked Nanase.

"Well, a-apparently the winners always go missing each year, and rumor has it their organs get sold on the black market..."

Organ trafficking? Such a thing was completely unheard of back in Japan, and the very thought of such a gruesome crime being commonplace only served to drive home how different this world really was.

"Why only the winners, though?" asked Hosoyama as she rubbed Tsuda's back to calm him down.

It was a good question. A beautiful woman's organs would be indiscernible from a plain woman's, no?

"Uh, well, the guys at the Guild said that organs from young and beautiful people sell for obscenely high prices on the black market, for whatever reason," Tsuda answered.

There was no such thing as a police force in this world. Back in Yamato, there was a faux-Shinsengumi band of neighborhood watchmen devoted to maintaining public order, but even that was a group of volunteers not officially affiliated with the local government. The governments of this world would take action if their sovereignty were ever put in danger, but they didn't do much when it came to things like thefts, murders, and abductions. This lawlessness was a bit more understandable in a world full of monsters that seemed to constantly be at war, but one would think they could at least do *something* about the rampant crime. There were plenty of assassination and revenge requests posted at the Adventurer's Guild, though most adventurers wouldn't dare take on that sort of work. Cold-blooded murder was still pretty taboo in this world, and few wanted to bloody their own hands on someone else's behalf. Not unless they were in desperate need of money, at the very least.

"What would you have us do, Satou?" I asked.

He took his time in answering me; it seemed like there was something about this particular subject he was trying to mull over very carefully. When he answered, it was with measured words. "You said the festival's being held in Uruk, correct? You don't think that villain Akira and Crow were talking about might be involved, do you? Gram, was it?"

Right, the guildmaster of the Uruk branch, and the man Crow's been trying to get revenge against for the past hundred years.

"Gee, I wonder," Hosoyama joked despondently. Indeed, one would think a man with such a laundry list of criminal activity would be bound to dip his toes in organ trafficking sooner or later.

"Well, whether it's him or not, it's still not okay," Waki added, and Satou nodded in agreement.

"We might not be in a position to judge how big a threat the demons and monsters pose to us right now, but we *are* in a position to judge that no one has the right to sell off another person's body. If it turns out this Gram guy *is* involved, then Crow will probably want in, and if Crow's in, that means Akira probably will be too... Don't get me wrong, the festival sounds fun, but this also sounds like the perfect opportunity for us to catch whoever's behind these crimes and prove to Akira and Princess Amelia beyond a shadow of a doubt that we're companions who know how to get stuff done."

With this final decree from Satou, our next course of action was decided.

POV: ODA AKIRA

"A FESTIVAL?! Are you out of your minds?!"

I couldn't help sounding hysterical. I was so taken aback by the statement that I accidentally knocked over the water bucket I was using to wash my face. I knew the hero and his party had been talking things over last night while I was out in the forest with Amelia, because the light in the room assigned to them was on even after we got home. But I never would have expected them to invite us to a festival first thing the next morning.

Kyousuke, who'd floated the idea to me, picked up the bucket I'd knocked over and started refilling it. "No, we're quite sane. It's being held over in Uruk, and it's quite famous from what we hear. Wouldn't it be worthwhile to take a look?" he said, wearing his best poker face.

I took the bucket back from him and furrowed my brow. "Uruk, huh?"

That was where the man we suspected had summoned the demons was residing—the same demons who had tried to kidnap Amelia. I *did* still want to pay him back for that. At the very least, I wanted to make him wish he'd never been born. I leaned over the bucket and splashed some water on my face, which helped to wake up my still-drowsy brain.

"You and Night are both well enough to travel, but not well

enough to fight, right? Obviously, training is important, but why not take a load off every once in a while?"

I mulled over Kyousuke's suggestion. I had no idea what the festivals in this world were like, but I had no doubt they'd be perfectly enjoyable. And if they were anything like Japan's festivals, then there'd be plenty of yummy food, which I knew Amelia would love. The only thing concerning me was whether Kyousuke had some ulterior motive for this recreational detour.

"What are you scheming?" I asked as I dried my face with my sleeve. He couldn't possibly know about Amelia's legendary appetite, so he clearly wasn't trying to win her over with festival food. Was there something else about this festival making him so determined to go? I looked at him quizzically and he simply chuckled.

"I think you're being a bit too suspicious. Not that I blame you, given that you just nearly escaped death's doorstep. Believe me, there's nothing deeper to it. The girls in our party really wanted to go, and so we thought Princess Amelia might be interested as well. It will give us some time to think about how to best convince her to let us join you."

It was true; I had grown a lot more suspicious after having lived in this world for a while, but being distrustful was almost a necessity in this world, where one wrong move could get you killed.

After a moment's deliberation, I said, "Consider us tentatively interested, then. I still need to ask Amelia and Night about it, but I think they'll probably be on board."

I also wanted a chance to ask Crow what festivals in this world were like. My face washed and my head clear, I began to put together my plans for the day.

Unbeknownst to me, Kyousuke flashed a satisfied smirk.

"A festival?!"

Amelia and Night were about as shocked by the idea as I'd been. The only difference between them was that Night was immediately opposed to the idea, while Amelia seemed delighted.

"Master, this wouldn't happen to be the upcoming beauty pageant festival being held in Uruk, would it?" asked Night.

"Hell if I know. All I know is that it's in Uruk... Wait a minute. You mean they have beauty pageants in this world too?"

"Wait, so we're going to it?! Oh, can we?! Pretty please?!" Amelia asked, her eyes lighting up as she grabbed my hand.

"Y-yeah, I figured you'd wanna go, so I told them we were tentatively interested... What's so great about this festival, though?" I asked.

"I have no idea!" She beamed, and I couldn't help but slump my shoulders.

"Why are you so excited to go, then?"

"I mean, it's a *festival*, right? There's bound to be all sorts of food and goodies!"

So it really was all about the food for her, then. Couldn't say I didn't expect that, though it was kind of cute to see her get all excited like this. I looked down at Night, who was standing up on his hind legs and facepalming with both hands.

"Master, Lady Amelia, please. They call that thing a festival, but it's really just a glorified all-out brawl. Though there are *plenty of excellent food stands, to be sure."*

"Are you saying you've been to this festival, Night?"

"Indeed. And not that long ago, actually."

And so Night proceeded to give us the rundown of what the beauty pageant festival truly entailed. Apparently, it had begun in Kantinen many years ago, but it was now so large that the human continent traded off hosting duties with Brute every other year. The pageant itself was divided into both a men's and a women's competition, though entrants were free to sign up as whichever gender they liked, and crossdressing was fully allowed. The pageant was traditionally only open to humans and beastfolk, though there had been a surprise upset victory by an elven competitor a few years back. Also, the winners always received a fabulous grand prize, which changed every year—last year, it was a free lifetime pass to one of the finest traditional inns in all of Kantinen. Since the pageant was being held in Uruk this year, word on the street was that the prize might be something more related to fine cuisine this time around. Upon hearing this, a fire ignited in Amelia's eyes.

"That's it. Sign me up," she declared, clenching her fists.

"...Master?" Night asked, looking to me with the hope that I could talk her out of it. I shook my head. Once Amelia had set her heart on something, there could be no stopping her.

"Why did you describe it as an 'all-out brawl,' though?" I asked. If it was really so dangerous, then I wasn't about to let her enter, even if it meant incurring her wrath.

"Well, you know how rowdy men can get... When the winner gets announced and it's not any of the women the crowd was pulling for, things can get violent rather quickly," he explained. This I could see.

"I'm gonna win that grand prize, Akira," Amelia asserted, as though she hadn't heard what Night said.

Night and I looked at each other, then shook our heads, exasperated.

"Well, I certainly find it hard to imagine that there could be anyone more beautiful than you, Amelia. She'd probably be a shoo-in, don't you think?" I asked Night.

"...Probably so."

"You guys are headed to the festival in Uruk? Seriously?"

Crow seemed just as taken aback by the idea as the rest of us had initially. It made sense; most people who had just barely escaped from a close encounter with demons probably wouldn't be raring to go to a festival the next day. If I were in Crow's shoes, I'd probably ask our group to get the hell out of my house.

"Do you wanna come with?" I ventured, and Crow went silent and looked away.

Uruk was the country where his sister's killer resided. I didn't know why he hadn't already gone and tried to exact revenge before now, but I could certainly understand why he might have reservations.

"You're serious about this?" he asked.

"Completely. Amelia really wants to go. She's all about good food, as you know."

Crow gave a little nod of understanding and then looked up at the night sky with the same vacant eyes as the night before. And just like last night, it was only the two of us sitting in his living room. I let out a sigh.

The hero's party had gone out to assist with the city's reconstruction efforts, and Amelia, Night, and Gilles had headed out at the same time to gather additional foodstuffs in the nearby mountains. This was a necessity now that we had so many mouths to feed, but I wasn't feeling well enough to go mountain climbing just yet, so I'd stayed behind to hold down the fort with Crow. The silence in the room was almost unbearable, though, so I'd decided to broach the subject of the festival and ask if Crow wanted to come along.

Amelia had told me all about how Crow and Night first met, as well as the unfortunate circumstances surrounding his sister's death. Being an older brother myself, I could definitely sympathize with the feelings he was struggling with. No matter how much you might bicker and fight with your siblings, family was still family. Although, since Yui and I were twins born just minutes apart, I realized we might have grown up to be closer than your average siblings.

She probably doesn't really even think of me as an older brother, and she's always believed that the doctor mixed us up and that she's actually the older sibling. Whenever she's forced to introduce me as her older brother, it's like pulling teeth for her, heh. But to me, she'll always be my adorable little sister, no matter how feisty she can be. If someone ever took her life, there's no way I'd be able to stop myself.

I'd use whatever means I could, no matter how illegal, to make the bastard pay. Obviously, I haven't been through what Crow's been through, but surely he must feel the same way about his sister, right?

"You're wondering why I haven't gone after my sister's murderer even though I know who he is, aren't you?" Crow asked, his tail moving to and fro. This snapped me right out of my thoughts. He turned his gaze away from the window and looked into my eyes, but there wasn't the slightest flicker of light in those obsidian pupils of his. "I can tell exactly what's going through your mind. You might have a pretty good poker face, but your eyes say more than your mouth ever could."

It was easy to forget that this man had more than a century of life experience over me—probably due in no small part to the fact he didn't look a day older than Gilles on the outside.

"There are two main reasons," Crow began, his expression calm. "First, because I know my sister would never have wanted me to sully my hands with the blood of our fellow beastmen. And second..." Crow paused, then slammed his fists down against his knees in vexation. "I'm too old to fight for extended periods like I used to. You humans might not be able to comprehend this, but old age hits us beastfolk without warning. You could be feeling spry and lively one day, then wake up the next unable to even pull yourself out of bed. Happens to people all the time."

Interesting. So there was a beastfolk-specific aging phenomenon. This was news to me.

"Obviously, it varies from person to person, but for me it came on pretty fast," Crow continued. "After my sister died,

I immediately started gathering all the intel I could on Gram and spent close to fifty years plotting my revenge, but by the time I was finally ready to put the plan into action, I was already an old fart. I think it probably hit me extra hard too, because of all the wild adventuring I did in my younger years."

Crow flashed a self-deprecating smile. It sounded like Gram was a lucky bastard; either that, or Crow was extremely unlucky.

"You know that staff of Lia's? I made that for her, way back before she was adopted into the royal family, since I knew she was gonna grow up to be a fine guardian one day. Finest staff I ever crafted. Got a very special mana stone embedded in it, and that's what tipped me off to you being in mortal danger down in the labyrinth... Though I've gotta admit, I did think twice about whether I really wanted to save your butts."

That meant we owed our survival to Lia as much we owed it to Crow. They must have known each other for quite a while. What *was* their relationship, exactly?

"But see, there's a reason I came to save you. You know what that is?" Crow asked, derailing my train of thought. He looked uncharacteristically serious about this, as evidenced by the fire of emotion now burning in his eyes.

I gulped. "What?"

"Well..." Crow began, his lips curling into the faintest of smirks.

A few days later, we arrived in the country of Uruk ready to begin our little vacation, and no worse for wear from the journey.

The city where they were hosting the festival (Mali, I believe) was among the largest in the nation. A giant stage was being constructed in the central plaza, and people in other towns all across Uruk would be able to watch the action via some sort of magic that sounded a lot like TV broadcasting. It wasn't just Mali livening up for the festivities either—the entire country was abuzz and ready to get in on the action. There were food stands all along the road leading into the city, many of which had come all the way from Kantinen to sell their local cuisines.

The crowds were pretty unbearable. Even before we made it into the city proper, it felt like we were being crammed into a can of sardines. Only Mali residents and the actual pageant entrants were allowed within the city limits. I couldn't blame the local officials for instating the rule, given the size of the crowds. Occasionally, I noticed people wearing flashy outfits—who I assumed were hopeful contestants—as well as plenty of folks who were just sitting on the sidelines, likely feeling overwhelmed by the sheer number of people.

"Look, Akira! There are so many foods I've never even heard of!" cried Amelia.

We were garnering a fair bit of attention just walking down the street. Our merry band certainly made for quite the sight— me, Amelia, Night, and the hero's party all walking together down the main drag. Incidentally, Crow hated crowds, so he was staying off the beaten path with Gilles.

What surprised me more than anything, however, was that people didn't seem to be focusing on Amelia, the princess dual-wielding fatty foods in both hands with childlike glee, but on me. At first, I couldn't imagine why, but then I heard a group of bystanders talking among themselves, and it all made sense:

"Hey...isn't that the Silent Assassin?"

"Wait a minute. Are you kidding me?! I thought he was just an urban legend!"

"The one who cleared a city block of monsters in half a second! You think he'd give me his autograph?"

Not a chance, I answered internally. I still couldn't believe it; how on earth was an assassin supposed to do his job if the average person recognized him on sight? I didn't ask to be a celebrity, darn it. And how did these people even know it was me, for that matter? Maybe it was the combination of black eyes and black hair, which wasn't especially common in Morrigan.

"Are you famous or something, Akira? Maybe I should ask you for an autograph sometime too," said Kyousuke, who was walking beside me. I groaned. His cluelessness could be frustrating at times.

"I don't give autographs, you idiot. Now make yourself useful and help me hide."

"Are you sure? Well, okay, then." Kyousuke stepped in front of me so I could walk in his shadow. Unfortunately, this wasn't enough to fully conceal me from the crowd.

"Hey, let's go try to say hi!"

"Oh my god, can we?!"

"I'm coming too!"

"Please, no..." I grumbled.

"Why not just conceal your presence, Master? I don't see a better way out of this for you," said Night, who was riding on Amelia's shoulder.

I nodded, having no problem with that idea aside from one small thing. "Okay, but you have to take care of Amelia for me."

"But of course."

The street was so flooded with pedestrians that I couldn't easily conceal my presence without bumping into people. This meant I would have to jump up and walk along the roofs of the food stands lining the street—which wasn't a problem, but it meant I wouldn't be able to easily leap to Amelia's aid if something bad happened. There had already been plenty of lowlifes catcalling her, so I was reluctant to leave her side. Having a black cat like Night on her shoulders was enough to deter most beastfolk from approaching her (given the whole "Nightmare of Adorea" thing), but most humans probably saw the cat as the perfect icebreaker.

"Kyousuke, I'm gonna step away from the group for a little while. I want you to keep an eye on Amelia for me. If any wise guys try to make a move on her, feel free to knock them into next week," I said.

"Got it." Kyousuke nodded.

I activated Conceal Presence, and all the older girls who'd been running my way for an autograph balked. Judging by their stunned expressions, I'd successfully turned invisible. I leapt onto the roof of a nearby food stand. Unlike the Japanese food stands I was used to, they all seemed to be made out of sturdy wood, so

I could be fairly certain of my footing. The whole country had been waiting for this day for a long time, so it made sense that they'd had a lot of time to set these up.

"Hey, look, y'all! A target practice game!" said Ueno, noticing a festival game stand a little farther down the road.

It didn't use BB guns like the ones back in Japan. Instead, it seemed to make use of wind magic so that any willing contestant could give it a shot. You simply aimed a device that looked kind of like a stick at the prize you wanted, channeled a tiny bit of mana into it, and a high-velocity wind bullet came shooting out. If you were successful, the prize would fall and you could take it home. It was all a matter of precision and mana control.

"Hey, little lady! Wanna try yer luck?" asked the staffer running the stand.

"You bet I do!" shouted Ueno, who immediately forked over the cash and picked up the shooting device with a grin. "Let's do this! Hey, Amelia, you see any prizes you want?"

"Hmm... That bag of candies sure looks nice," Amelia commented.

Ueno and Amelia had become fast friends since we began our journey to Uruk. Maybe they'd both gotten caught up in the infectious festival spirit. Come to think of it, I remembered them coming home together the day Crow and I were left alone back at the house while everyone else went off to do things. Maybe that was when they first became friends. In any case, I was glad to see Amelia enjoying herself. I knew being a princess made it pretty hard for her to have normal friendships.

"Aim carefully now, Ueno."

"You betcha! And...take that! Ohhh!"

The prize fell to the ground, and Amelia's face lit up.

"Lookit that, y'all! Your girl's still got it!"

"Nice shot, little lady... Here ya go! Take this one too! On the house!" said the employee.

"Aw, shucks! That's awful kind of you, mister!"

Amelia looked so happy to get the candies from Ueno that I couldn't help but crack a smile. I was starting to feel very happy that we'd decided to come to this festival. It was almost enough to make me forget the bloodbath from only a few days prior.

As we made our way down the main road, stopping at any stalls that suited our fancy, we eventually arrived at Mali proper, and the site of the beauty pageant. With Amelia stopping at every food stand offering something she'd never tried before, and Ueno and Waki eating up a bunch of time playing festival games, we made it to the city just in time for the festival to officially start (we were planning to arrive with plenty of time to spare, for the record).

After watching from a bird's-eye view, I was now utterly convinced that Amelia's stomach had to be some sort of black hole. Since we arrived, she'd had both her hands occupied with a constant rotation of food that she inhaled fast enough to deter any would-be pick-up artists from hitting on her. Kyousuke, bless his heart, stuck by her side through it all in honor of my wishes, but even he couldn't help but wince at the sight.

"Well, that was quite the ordeal," Crow grumped as we entered the city limits and finally escaped the suffocating crowds.

Now the only people around us were pageant contestants and their attendants, so we could see more than clustered bodies around us. Granted, there was no gated entry or anything, so there were a few stragglers, but there weren't many food stands or attractions set up within Mali to avoid overcrowding. There were still a lot of people, but we could at least make out Crow and Gilles as they walked over to rejoin the rest of the party.

"Oh, don't be such a spoilsport! It's a festival! The whole point is to let loose and enjoy yourself!" said Amelia as she hoovered down the last few bites of the remaining treats in her hands.

At this point, I jumped down beside her and deactivated Conceal Presence. "Well, let's head on over to the venue. Still too many prying eyes around here," I said, ignoring the surprised faces of the hero's party members startled by my sudden reappearance.

Amelia was finally finished eating, so her beautiful face was beginning to shine through once more—which meant she was now subjected to jealous glares from other women who were clearly planning to enter the pageant, as well as lurid glances from the men I could only assume were attendants. Amelia was used to this kind of attention, so it didn't faze her, but as her boyfriend, I couldn't allow it to continue.

"Speaking of which, who all is planning to enter?" I asked.

Amelia, Hosoyama, Ueno, and the hero all raised their hands.

"Ain't often you get the chance to enter a real-life beauty pageant! Sounds mighty fun to me!" said Ueno, ever the optimist.

"I always kind of wanted to try being a model," said Hosoyama, who did indeed have the body for it.

"Sweet! This triples our chances of winning the grand prize!" said Amelia, who apparently didn't care who won as long as she got to enjoy the prize. I took a quick look over at the hero, who was scratching his nose sheepishly.

"Er... Y-yeah, I kinda thought it'd be fun to try too! And by having someone in the men's competition, that means we have yet another chance to win the grand prize. But don't worry, Amelia— if it's food-related, I'll be sure to give it to you," he said.

"You mean it?!" she chirped, her eyes aglow.

"Um, yeah, for sure..." he said, clearly a little taken aback by the sheer magnitude of her gluttony.

At long last, we reached the front of the registration line.

"Okay, anyone who wants to enter, please sign right here and provide some form of identification. Any escorts or chaperones, please do the same," said the lady at the registration table. We all opted to show our Adventurer's Guild dog tags, since that was the easiest and only form of identification we really had in this world. I couldn't help but feel like security was fairly lax if all it took to register was an ID and a signature. But when it was Amelia's turn to show her dog tags, the registration lady suddenly seized up.

"Wait, what? Erm, sorry, just one moment please!" she sputtered.

Well, guess I can't blame her for being surprised. It's not every day that elven royalty stops by, I thought as she turned around to call for her superior. Amelia had gotten a lot of attention for her good looks while we were in the beastfolk domain, but there probably weren't many people here who could recognize her as princess of the elves from appearance alone. Few elves ever traveled beyond the borders of the Sacred Forest, so it wasn't like her face was well known to the general public, even if her name and class as a spirit medium apparently were.

"Th-thank you so much for your patience, Princess Amelia," said the man who'd dashed over, presumably the other woman's supervisor. He was forcing a polite smile, but his eyes were scanning Amelia's body from top to bottom. "I do apologize for the inconvenience, but do you have a secondary form of identification we could use to confirm that you are indeed Her Highness Amelia, Princess of the Elves? We've had to really tighten our security in recent years, because we *do* get the odd impostor from time to time, I'm afraid."

In other words, they weren't buying that she was who she said she was. But in a competition of looks, did her title really buy her that much of an advantage?

"And what benefit would an Amelia imposter get, might I ask?" said Kyousuke, apparently having wondered the same thing.

The man was now sweating profusely, but still trying to maintain his customer service façade. "W-well, I don't fully understand the rationale myself, to be quite honest with you, but we do call all contestants by name before they walk out on stage, so bigger names tend to draw more attention; I'm sure you understand."

That made sense. With the sheer number of contestants, something like that could definitely help someone stand out from the crowd.

"Very well," said Amelia. "Will this be sufficient?"

She held out the envelope that had contained a letter from the king of the elves addressed to Lingga, and it still had the king's personal seal stamped in wax on the back. Apparently, she'd gotten the envelope back from Lingga at some point.

The moment the man saw the seal, his facial expression shifted and he started bowing his head repeatedly. "A-apologies for having doubted you, Your Highness! Please do enjoy the festival to your heart's content!"

The men's and women's competitions were to be held simultaneously, and while I had no interest in watching the men's competition, especially since the hero was entering, I couldn't shake the feeling that he and my fellow classmates were hiding something. The only person in the group I knew well enough to try probing for answers was Kyousuke, but unfortunately he had the best poker face of anyone I knew. At the same time, I could tell the more easy-to-read members of the group like Ueno and Waki were getting pretty antsy as the pageant was about to begin.

"Well, see you guys later," said the hero. The men's competition was being held somewhere deeper in the city. It wasn't nearly as popular as the women's competition, so it was much less of a popularity contest and more a collection of average dudes just hoping to take home the prize. Apparently, the footage of the event being "broadcast" to other cities focused almost exclusively on the female portion as well.

"Yup, good luck out there," I said.

Waki, Nanase, and Tsuda went along with the hero to cheer him on, while the women, Kyousuke, and I stayed behind. Something still felt a bit off to me about all this, mind you, but before I had time to consider it, our attention was forcibly drawn to commotion near the entrance of the venue.

"I already told ya! My name's Latty, and I'm a demon who came all the way from Volcano to enter your stupid pageant! What more do you people want from me?!"

A hooded girl was kicking up quite a fuss over at the registration counter, and once my brain actually had a chance to process the words she was saying, I froze up.

"A demon...?" Here in broad daylight, making a giant scene? I turned to look at Night on Amelia's shoulders, only to see his mouth hanging wide open.

The girl's purple eyes peeked out from under her hood as she threw her fists toward the sky in protest, not even caring about the dirty looks she was getting. She looked like a child throwing a tantrum. "What's the big idea here, huh?! You'll let humans and beastfolk participate, and even a freakin' elven *princess*, but one little demon is where you draw the line?! This is racism!"

"W-well, you see, erm..." said a pageant official, this one sweating even more profusely than the last as he stumbled over his words. He was looking around desperately for someone to help him, but the other representative was clearly still feeling frazzled from his interaction with Amelia, and the new guy let out a heavy sigh when he realized he was on his own.

"Let's go over there, Night."

"M-Master?"

I grabbed Night by the scruff of his neck and headed toward the entrance. The pageant official, upon further inspection, was a rabbitlike beastfolk. I originally thought he just had long white hair, but it was actually a pair of long floppy ears hanging down the sides of his face. I always assumed rabbits were skittish animals, so I was surprised to see one in a position of authority. I could also see his little poofy bunny tail wiggling anxiously right above his tailbone. *A fat man with bunny ears... Now I've truly seen it all.*

"What seems to be the problem here?" I asked, with Night still dangling from my fingers. Immediately, the bunnyman's eyes lit up, seeing a life raft to help him out of this situation. Before he could say a word, though, the hooded girl grabbed my free hand and started begging me to hear her out.

"Hey, you! Do *you* think I shouldn't be allowed to participate just 'cause I'm a demon? If even a random bystander says I shouldn't be able to, then I guess I have no choice but to give up." She was standing so close to me that my eyes couldn't help but be drawn down to her breasts—which were a fair bit bigger than Amelia's.

I could feel Amelia's eyes burning a hole in the back of my head, so I decided I'd better solve this problem, and fast. "I don't see any reason you shouldn't be allowed to enter," I muttered, trying desperately to avert my gaze from her buxom chest. With this, the hooded girl did a triumphant fist pump, and the bunnyman looked at me like I'd just sentenced him to death.

"B-but that's simply unheard of! It's unprecedented! Never in the history of this pageant has there ever been a demon contestant, and, and—"

"Everything's unprecedented until someone dares to be the first. Besides, she seems pretty harmless. If she tries to start trouble, I'll be happy to put her in her place."

My Detect Danger skill wasn't picking up anything from her, and she wasn't giving off an exorbitant mana aura either. Certainly nothing the average citizen couldn't handle. I was fairly confident I could subdue her if she tried anything funny, and even if she *was* concealing her true abilities somehow, I could always ask Crow for help. There was no way this little girl could be any stronger than Mahiro, surely.

"Well, if you swear you'll keep an eye on her as one of the princess's retainers, I suppose... B-but if anything goes wrong, I'm holding you accountable!" the bunnyman said, before retreating back to his post.

"Guess this means you're coming with us now. You got that?" I asked the girl.

She nodded excitedly, her purple eyes glimmering with hope from underneath her hood. She had such a different vibe compared to Aurum Tres and Mahiro Abe that I honestly found it hard to believe this spunky little girl could be a demon. Sure, she seemed every bit as mischievous and childish as Aurum had, but she didn't seem to be at all messed up like him.

"Yup, works for me!" she replied, then squinted at Night dangling from my grip. "Hey, wait a minute. Don't I know you from somewhere, kitty-cat?"

"Y-yes, um... It's a pleasure to make your acquaintance again, Lady Latticenail," Night said. Now this I was not expecting. Given that Night had been the Demon Lord's right-hand pet, I'd always assumed his status among demon society had been quite high. So his use of honorifics with this girl implied she wasn't just any ordinary demon.

"Right, now I remember! You're Black Cat, aren't ya? What the heck are you doin' *here*, of all places?" the demon girl asked, and Night's eyes began to waver.

"Erm, yes, well... About that..."

As Night fumbled over his words, the purple-haired girl's eyes narrowed as if she'd come up with a brilliant new prank. "Oh, *I* get it... I had a feeling you wouldn't just let yourself get killed down there, but I wasn't expecting you to make a pact with a freakin' *human*, of all things. Does Dad know about this?"

Dad? I wondered as Night nodded, anguished.

Then Latticenail sized me up for a minute before giving Night's head a friendly scratch. "Welp, okay then! In that case, I'll keep my mouth shut. Nice to meet you, little kitty I've never met before—what's your name?"

"Hello, young lady. My name is Night. I'm this boy's familiar."

"Night, huh? That's a pretty cute name."

"I'm flattered."

While Night seemed quite relieved at this turn of events, I felt like I was being completely ignored. Suddenly, I could relate to how Gilles felt around Commander Saran. After exchanging false felicitations, the two of them finally looked up at me.

"Welp, we're here now, so we might as well enjoy the festival, right?" Latticenail grinned as she dragged me off by the hand before I even had a chance to ask Night what the hell was going on. The little kitty looked up at me with an ever-so-slightly pained expression on his face.

"I promise I'll explain later. To you and Lady Amelia both."

Amelia had planted herself not too far away, her arms crossed and her cheeks puffed in a pout. I flashed her a sheepish grin.

"C'mon, Amelia. Don't be mad," I said. At this, she promptly turned away. Apparently, she really wasn't taking a liking to this Latticenail girl who'd suddenly apprehended me.

"I'm not mad," Amelia huffed. "I don't have anything against the girl whatsoever; she seems like a pretty good person, actually. I just don't like that you're being so flirty with her."

"What? I'm not being flirty at all. Please don't misunderstand me... Wait a minute. What do you mean, she seems like a good person?" I asked.

"She may be a demon, but I don't sense any malice from her," Amelia said over her shoulder. "Besides, did you even check her stats?"

I snapped my fingers, having forgotten I even had that ability. I'd sworn to only use World Eyes when absolutely necessary, so I generally didn't check other people's stats unless I was facing them in battle. But there was reason to be wary of this girl, so I quickly corrected that oversight and activated World Eyes to take a peek at her stats.

LATTICENAIL

RACE: Demon	**CLASS:** Water/Fire Mage (Lv. 57)
HP: 33000/33000	**MP:** 44000/44000
ATTACK: 38500	**DEFENSE:** 33000

SKILLS:

Water Magic (Lv. 6)	Fire Magic (Lv. 6)
Mesmerize (Lv. 8)	

EXTRA SKILLS:

Monster Control	Mana Suppression

I couldn't help but rub my eyes in disbelief at the stats I was seeing. Granted, numbers so high from a demon weren't all that unbelievable anymore after having seen Aurum Tres's stats, but in Latticenail's case, the numbers just didn't seem to match up with my first impressions of her. How could this mischievous and seemingly harmless girl, who was currently waving happily to all the other pageant contestants, have higher stats overall than even Aurum Tres, despite being a lower level? Maybe her Mana Suppression Extra Skill was making her mana aura completely imperceptible, when, by rights, it should have been suffocating everyone in the entire venue. And to think I wouldn't have even bothered to check if Amelia hadn't pointed it out to me.

"You really do need to get in the habit of using World Eyes more often, Akira," Amelia chided me.

I looked away, grumpy. "Well, yeah, but..."

Sure, World Eyes was a very handy ability—being able to sneak a peek at an enemy's stats was an advantage few in this world were lucky to have—but I could never forget the traumatic experience I had when I first tried it out. Though I didn't remember everything I'd seen in vivid detail, I still relived it in my nightmares from time to time. An image of Kyousuke's and the other heroes' lifeless bodies scattered across the rocky earth, and the only one left, standing right in the middle of them all... was me. I didn't know if it was supposed to be a vision of a future that would inevitably come to pass, or just one possibility out of many, but I was deathly afraid to find out. And I probably *could* find out by using World Eyes again, if I really wanted to, but I wasn't sure I could handle it if it turned out I was destined to kill my classmates.

"Remember, we both see different things through World Eyes, so I can't know what exactly you're seeing or what might be concerning you, but the fact that you just assumed that girl was harmless when she was really just concealing her powers was a dangerous oversight on your part."

Amelia was right. Now that I'd seen the girl's stats, I realized it was irresponsible of me to promise I'd take care of her if she tried anything funny, because there was a good chance she was too powerful for me to handle. Thankfully, Crow was here too, so we could probably work together if it came to that, but what if he hadn't come with us?

"You're right. It was stupid of me to cover for her," I admitted with a sigh.

"No, you made the right call," Amelia said, shaking her head. "She very well could have gotten violent if you hadn't stepped in and made them accept her registration. All I was trying to say was that you've got eyes that can see things no one else can—so you should use them."

There was a calm, almost motherly affection in Amelia's deep red eyes.

"I hear you. I'll be sure to check the stats of anyone I meet for the first time from now on," I assured her, and she nodded before standing up on her tippy-toes to give me a few pats on the head. It was a pretty cute gesture, I had to admit.

"Ahem! Master, Lady Amelia? Can I speak to you two for a moment?" asked Night, butting into our little intimate moment before leaping up onto my shoulders; he probably wanted to tell us more about Latticenail.

"So? Who is that hooded demon girl, anyway? The way you were talking all formally to her, I have to assume she's someone important," I theorized. Night nodded, then cast a sidelong glance over to where Latticenail was standing.

"Lady Latticenail is... Well, to put it bluntly, she's His Majesty's daughter."

Oh, is that all? I nodded a few times before this information truly sank in, then froze in place. *Wait a minute. She's the Demon Lord's daughter?!*

"Well...based purely on her stats, I can believe it, but she sure doesn't look the part," said Amelia, and I couldn't agree more. Maybe it had something to do with how we couldn't feel her mana whatsoever, or maybe it had something to do with her innocent, childlike behavior, but she sure didn't seem like a daughter of the

Demon Lord to me. Hell, I was still having a hard time believing the Demon Lord even *had* a daughter.

"Well, Lady Latticenail and His Majesty don't get along very well, and they're constantly fighting over one thing or another. I'm guessing she probably ran away from home again after getting in another screaming match with him. And, well...as you can see, she doesn't really have the kind of personality that befits the daughter of a Demon Lord."

I wouldn't have gone quite *that* far, but it was true that she certainly didn't act like I expected a demon would. Was he implying that she ran away to a completely different continent, though? Was that normal for demon teenagers going through rebellious phases?

"In any event, I'm sure things will be fine so long as you never lie to Lady Latticenail's face, and never use discriminatory language or racist slurs when addressing her. Those are the two things she hates more than anything else."

Right—she'd kicked up a huge fuss about the festival officials being racist for not letting her register earlier, hadn't she? I was pretty sure I'd even heard her say something about how "Daddy says there's nothing worse than a racist." If she was referring to the Demon Lord...maybe I needed to reevaluate my preconceptions of the guy.

"Thanks, I'll keep that in mind." I nodded. "And I'll make sure Kyousuke and the others know too."

"A good idea, Master. I'll stay here with Lady Amelia. Just be careful not to get on Lady Latticenail's bad side," warned Night,

before hopping off of my shoulders and onto Amelia's. Evidently, he was determined to spend as little time with Latticenail as possible.

CHAPTER 2

The Beauty Pageant

POV: ODA AKIRA

BEFORE I KNEW IT, the competition had begun. Apparently, Amelia, Latticenail, and the girls from the hero's party were among the last entrants to register; as such, they'd be among the last to appear on stage. With Latticenail chattering excitedly by my side, I watched the event play out from the venue floor. So far, all of the contestants had been either human or beastfolk, and there were certainly some good-looking entrants among them, but since I got to spend every day with an unmatched beauty like Amelia, none of them really made a huge impression on me. Based on facial features alone, something told me Amelia would have no problem wiping the floor with any of these girls...though there *was* one contestant whose face I hadn't seen yet, come to think of it.

"So hey, are you gonna take that hood off eventually, or what?" I asked, and Latticenail (who'd been watching the contestants with rapt attention) quickly turned to face me, squinting devilishly with her purple eyes.

"What, and ruin the surprise? If I took it off now, everyone would know I was bound to win the grand prize from the get-go, and where's the fun in that? Besides, haven't you ever heard of showmanship? I wanna make the crowd go wild!"

It sounded like she was awfully confident in her looks. Considering she'd already met Amelia and therefore knew what she was up against, she either had to be the most beautiful girl in all of Morrigan, or she was just blowing smoke. Given her personality, I could see it being the latter, but on the off chance that it was the former, I was very interested to see her beauty for myself.

"Whassa matter, big guy? Has little ol' Latty caught your eye? Better be careful, or you might just wanna dump that elf princess for me!" she snickered, and I promptly flicked her on the forehead. Even if she *was* more beautiful than Amelia, for the sake of argument, it wasn't like I loved Amelia for her looks alone, and I could say with 100 percent confidence I could never fall for someone with a personality like Latticenail's. "God, you two really are obnoxiously head over heels for each other, huh? I'm surprised Night hasn't gone off the deep end from having to watch your PDAs yet."

I let out an awkward laugh. *Little does she know.*

POV: ASAHINA KYOUSUKE

O NE BY ONE, the contestants strode across the stage, and I had to admit, I was starting to feel increasingly anxious about this whole endeavor. Our plan to protect Princess Amelia while also exposing Gram's villainy was starting to feel impossible, and the sudden appearance of a demon girl wasn't helping matters. The original plan was to have myself and our female classmates close at hand so we could rush to Princess Amelia's aid if Gram tried anything funny after she won the competition, and to have Waki, Tsuda, and Nanase standing by at the men's competition for the same purpose if Satou won. It may have been an oversight to not have our entire force gathered around Princess Amelia, but at least Akira and Night were around and would help if need be.

Still, the main thing we needed to watch out for was Guildmaster Gram and his henchmen. According to Tsuda's intel, his henchmen would be adorned with the national crest of Uruk somewhere on their persons—a circle with three claws above it. But as I was scanning the crowd for any sign of this symbol, a demon by the name of Latticenail showed up to throw a wrench in our plans.

Assuming the rumors about Gram having made a deal with the demons were true, we had yet another potentially dangerous enemy to watch out for. It was all starting to give me quite the migraine, especially since Akira didn't seem to think she was a threat. He did warn us not to lie or use discriminatory language around her, but he appeared to trust this demon girl.

According to Night, while we were all twiddling our thumbs waiting for our boat to arrive in the beastfolk domain, Princess Amelia was kidnapped by the demons, and Akira risked life and limb to save her. He would have lost that gamble had it not been for a timely rescue by Crow. I couldn't believe Akira would so easily trust a member of the same race that nearly killed him mere days ago; it was too foolhardy to fathom. And try as I might to warn him, the demon in question was staying frustratingly close by his side, giving me no opportunity to speak with him in private.

"Y'all really think it's wise to trust that demon gal?" I overheard Ueno saying.

"Tsuda was saying most of the buyers who purchased the organs on the black market were demons too. I have to wonder if that's the real reason she came here," said Hosoyama. It seemed the two of them shared my primary concerns.

"So you two agree, then," I said in a low voice so Akira wouldn't overhear. The two girls nodded.

"I mean, the timing's just too dang fishy, y'know what I mean?"

"Asahina, why don't you leave Amelia to us and go keep a close eye on her and Oda?"

I nodded, having arrived at the same conclusion myself. It helped that Akira and I were friends, so it wouldn't be overly suspicious for me to want to hang out near him.

As I approached the pair, they were chatting rather amicably, but they quickly looked up to greet me.

"Oh, hey, Kyousuke. Looks like it's almost, uh...the girls' turns, yeah?"

I nodded. Ueno, Hosoyama, and Princess Amelia had already headed off toward the stage. I'd assumed it would take time for them to get through the line, but they were moving through it rather quickly. Apparently, a lot of the other contestants in their group had walked out after seeing Amelia's face. Which made sense—if there were any who could hope to match her beauty, I would have liked to see them. Speaking of which, I turned to address the hooded demon girl.

"Shouldn't you be on your way as well?" I asked.

The girl gasped as though she'd totally forgotten, then quickly scurried off toward the stage. After all, if Princess Amelia's turn was coming up, then hers would surely be soon to follow. I let out a halfhearted chuckle and moved to Akira's side, looking up at the stage along with him.

"I take it you forgot Hosoyama's and Ueno's names again, Akira?" I remarked, and he shuddered.

"Can't hide anything from you, can I?" He then offered a sheepish laugh.

"Of course not. You may not remember, but we've known each other for quite a long time, you and I." I *had* known him and Satou for well over ten years. To my surprise, Akira stopped laughing and looked at me with deadly seriousness in his eyes. A chill ran down my spine.

"Yeah, well. You can't hide anything from me either, big guy," he said. "And while it's true I don't usually pay much attention to other people, I *have* come to learn how to read your poker face a little bit... So tell me, Kyousuke—what exactly are you trying to pull here?"

"What are you talking about?"

These were not the eyes of a friend. I'd never seen Akira look at me like that back in Japan. I twisted my neck anxiously in an attempt to play it off, but his gaze only grew all the more suspicious.

"If you were trying to pull the wool over my eyes, you should've had the chick with the Kansai accent and the animal trainer guy go off somewhere I couldn't see. That girl's been fidgeting anxiously ever since the pageant began," he replied. He was right that Ueno and Waki were terrible at playing it cool, but having them go off on their own somewhere else would have only roused a different kind of suspicion. "And then there's you. You've been flustered ever since Latticenail arrived. I'll only ask you one more time: what are you planning? Or more specifically, what's about to happen here?"

I couldn't help but gasp—to think one of my best friends had the makings of a professional detective. Perhaps he was hypervigilant out of wariness after having nearly died not long ago. I slumped my shoulders and turned to look at Ueno, who was waving down at us from up on stage.

"I would be happy to tell you all about it, were it a plan I came up with on my lonesome, but I'm afraid this was the product of the entire party's brainstorming. I'm not at liberty to tell you any more than that," I answered. I hated having to lie to Akira, even if I knew it was for his own good. All I could do was hang my head and try my best to reassure him. "Something *is* going to happen here, and we're certain that it will draw Gram out of hiding...so be careful, Akira. And keep an eye on Princess Amelia."

"...All right."

POV: ODA AKIRA

I TOOK KYOUSUKE'S WARNING to heart and kept my eyes locked on Amelia to the best of my ability. Obviously, I couldn't keep an eye on her at all times, which was why I'd sent Night to keep tabs on her in the first place. Hearing Kyousuke say Gram's name made me very concerned about the degree to which Gram might be involved in this festival, but there was little I could do about it now, so I decided to try my best to enjoy the pageant.

"May I have your attention for entrant number 291! The one, the only...Princess Amelia!"

Right after the girl with the Kansai accent and the girl with the curvy bod came Amelia's turn. The venue immediately filled with noise; apparently, she was more well-known by the outside world than I'd thought. I could feel the anticipation building in the crowd before she even stepped out on the stage.

All eyes were on her when she finally revealed herself, garbed in a beautiful bright-green dress. Her silvery hair flowed in the air behind her as the spotlight illuminated her brilliant crimson eyes. With simple earrings adorning her pointy elven ears, her trademark features were on display. As every male jaw in the audience dropped one by one, I was among her admirers.

"You're gorgeous, Amelia," I whispered. I had to admit, I'd come to take her beauty ever so slightly for granted, just because I got to spend every day with her, but seeing her all dolled up made it a little hard to believe she was truly my girlfriend. I'd heard she had to borrow her dress since she was one of the final entrants to register. Our eyes met as she stood there up on the stage, and we smiled at each other. When she saw me looking on in amazement with all the other people in the audience, she gave me a coquettish little wink.

"WHOAAAAA!" the men in the audience cried.

Amelia walked to the end of the runway, did an about-face, then trotted back the way she came. The uproarious cheering continued until she vanished backstage.

"Ha ha... Guess it's true what they say about women being able to turn it on with the flip of a switch." I swooned, pressing my hands against my cheeks. To think she had been stuffing her face like a competitor in a hot dog-eating contest only a couple of hours ago, and now this? I could feel myself falling in love all over again. All of the women in the immediate vicinity were gushing excitedly about Amelia's beauty, while the men were still standing awestruck, looking up at the stage as though Amelia were still there. I wasn't sensing any fishy activity just yet.

"Looks like this pageant's really heating up, folks! Next up, entrant number 292! Give it up for Latty!"

Before the crowd had a chance to calm down, I looked up to see a still-hooded Latticenail walking out onto the stage, wearing a very confident smirk. A hush fell over the crowd. Everyone was watching with rapt attention, just waiting for the moment in which she'd unveil her true colors—myself included. I was very interested in seeing what the Demon Lord's daughter looked like.

After reaching center stage, she slowly brought her hands up to her cowl, and I heard an audible gulp ring out across the crowd. Then with a light thud, the cloak fell to the ground.

"Huh?" I uttered in disbelief.

"WHOAAAAA!" cried the audience.

Her eyes were like two beautiful amethysts, and while her layered outfit looked like something a female military officer might wear, her sublime proportions still shined through, her voluptuous thighs peeking enticingly out from beneath her skirt. Her face wasn't quite as stunning as Amelia's, but it was perfectly fine in its own right, and her loosely curled lavender hair was by far the most beautiful of any contestant—though perhaps it only made such an impression because she'd kept it hidden under a very plain frock.

If Amelia was a sculptor's vision of what the perfect elegant woman would be, Latticenail had the body of a voluptuous temptress that seemed far more realistic and human than an artist's ideal. If the question was which one was more likely to make the average guy drool, Latticenail took the cake, no question. And with all due respect to the other contestants, it was very clear the competition had just become a one-on-one battle between Amelia's pretty face and Latticenail's luscious curves. There hadn't been a single contestant yet who could hold a candle to either of them, and I didn't foresee any other last-minute contenders for the crown. If there *was* an even greater beauty waiting in the wings, I'd almost worry a large proportion of the crowd would die from frothing at the mouth.

"And that concludes the runway portion of this year's beauty pageant, folks! We'll now move onto the judging portion! If you're watching from one of our official viewing locations, please enter the number of your favorite contestant into one of our many voting panels! Remember, all you need to do is channel a tiny bit of mana into the panel, then write their number with your finger!"

As I listened to the announcer's instructions, I found the panel nearest me and began tapping away at it. Obviously, Amelia was getting my vote. After seeing the "vote received" confirmation message on the panel, I went to find Amelia backstage.

"Akira!"

"Hey, Amelia."

I found her in the waiting room backstage, where she and the nearly three hundred other female contestants were hanging out while they waited for the results to come in. Amelia was the only one who seemed to give off a radiant glow, even just by turning her head. By her side was Latticenail, with whom she'd been chatting amicably. I also noticed the two girls from the hero's party sitting nearby.

"Hey, mister! How'd I do?" asked Latticenail, running over to greet me with a friendly smile. She looked so excited, it almost felt like I could see a dog tail wagging behind her, though I had to be seeing things. "Seemed like you were preeetty curious about what I was hiding under my cloak. Any impressions you'd like to share?"

"Yeah, I was pretty impressed, I've gotta admit. Though you're still no match for Amelia," I clarified as I ruffled my girlfriend's hair. Amelia closed her eyes and purred contentedly. If Latticenail was secretly a dog, then Amelia could easily pass for a cat, and I was a diehard cat person.

Latticenail, unsatisfied with my response, placed her hands on her hips and puffed out her cheeks. "Well, yeah, no duh! Of course no one's gonna be better than Amelia! There's not another girl alive with a face like hers! But I mean, like... Not to toot my own horn or anything, but I know a lotta boys who'd kill for a chance with me!"

"Oh, Latty." Amelia chuckled. "You'd be perfectly cute if you just learned how to keep your mouth shut sometimes."

"Hey! Are you sayin' I'm a pretty girl with an ugly personality?!"

As I desperately fought the urge to nod my head, I marveled at how friendly the two of them had become in such a short period of time.

"Hey, that reminds me," said Latticenail, "I never did learn your name, did I, mister? I can't just keep callin' you 'mister' forever!"

Right, I guess I never did *introduce myself, did I?* I only knew her name thanks to Night and from her stat page. "Right, well then. Sorry for the belated introduction, but I'm Oda Akira. Or 'Akira Oda' in this world, I guess. Anyway, it's nice to meet you."

"Akira, huh? Okie-dokie! I'll be sure to remember that, mister!"

"She says, before immediately calling me 'mister' again..." I laughed halfheartedly. I decided it might be a good idea to learn what I could from her, especially since it seemed like it would be a while before the pageant results were announced. "So your full name's Latticenail, right? How come you registered as Latty, then? Is that just a nickname, or...?"

"Yup, I came up with it myself! Latticenail's just *so* long and unwieldy, y'know? I did consider just going by Lattice, but Latty's way cuter, don'tcha think?!"

It was true; "Lattice" sounded a bit too straight-laced for a spunky girl like her.

"Yeah, I like Latty better too," Amelia chimed in. "She and I have been talking this whole time, Akira. You wouldn't believe how funny this girl is!"

Amelia's expression softened, and I nodded in agreement. I could totally see how Latticenail's laid-back personality and way of speaking could help anyone feel more relaxed and at ease. There was a certain charisma about her that just drew people in.

"The results are in, folks! It's time for the moment you've all been waiting for—we're about to crown this year's champions!"

Everyone in the waiting room perked up as the announcement came in. I'd gotten so involved in my conversation with Latticenail that I'd forgotten the pageant wasn't actually over yet. She and Amelia turned to each other and smiled.

"Whoever wins, no hard feelings, okay?"

"Yup! Of course!"

According to the announcer, the top five contestants would be called back on stage. As all the other hopefuls in the waiting room clasped their hands in prayer, Amelia and Latticenail simply waited patiently for the results to be called out. While most entrants were probably just hoping for a spot in the top five, these two didn't care about anything but first place (though in Amelia's case, that was purely because she wanted the grand prize).

"So without further ado, it's time to announce our winners! In fifth place...entrant number 108, Natalia!"

A girl in a dark orange dress suddenly burst out in tears before heading directly for the stage, all the while muttering to herself, either out of happiness or disbelief.

"Next up, our fourth-place winner...entrant number 25, Aldylla!"

A crowlike beastgirl in a blue dress stood up with a huff and stomped over to the stage. Apparently unhappy with where she'd placed, she shot Amelia and Latticenail a dirty look on her way out. To be fair, were it not for them, she may have stood a real chance of taking home the grand prize. She *did* have a nice face, if you could look past her stuck-up personality.

"And in third place tonight... Give it up for entrant number 2! Sonora!"

A timid girl in a white dress stood up and looked around awkwardly before heading out. Maybe she'd won people over with her skittish, klutzy persona. With her departure, the vast majority of women left in the waiting area lowered their heads in defeat. Everyone with half a brain knew Amelia and Latticenail were bound to take the top two spots—it was just a question of who would come out on top.

"And now, let's hear it for this year's first-prize winners!"

"Huh?!" they both gasped.

"Oh, I see. So that's how it's gonna be," I said, realizing what it meant for second place to have been skipped entirely. Amelia and Latticenail shared a look that said they'd realized too.

"This is a historic moment, folks! For the first time in pageant history, we have a tie for first place! Give it up for entrants number 291 and 292, Princess Amelia and Latty!"

They'd both received the same number of votes, as unlikely as that seemed. As the announcer called out their names and the audience cheered, Amelia and Latticenail joined hands and headed back out to the stage.

"Now it's time to present our two winners with their awards and prizes!"

I exited the waiting room and took my place in front of the stage; I wanted to see the look on Amelia's face when they crowned her, and I couldn't do that from backstage. She was already up on the glimmering stage, waving down at me with a smile. I gave her a little smile back, though a lot of the men in my vicinity seemed to think she'd been waving at them and started hooting and hollering. Judging by the fact that the scene hadn't turned into an "all-out brawl" like Night described, I assumed most people in the audience were happy with the winners.

"W-well, let's welcome to the stage our grand-prize winners in the 256th annual beauty pageant, Princess Amelia and Latty. The two of you have earned our most auspicious award, and we will now honor you as such. My name is Lapin, and I'm chairman of the pageant committee."

The spotlight shined down on the two winners as they received their certificates from the very nervous-looking beastfolk representative who we had dealt with during registration—Lapin.

"Erm, as for the grand prize... I'm afraid it took a bit longer than expected to arrive, but you should be able to pick it up tomorrow. Is that all right with you both?"

Amelia nodded her head several times, her eyes aglimmer as she imagined what wondrous food items might be in store. We were going to stay in town for the night, then. I wondered if there were any vacant rooms left in the city.

Mali didn't really have the infrastructure for the kind of tourist surge that came with the pageant. I could only assume all of the rooms in town were already taken by human contestants who'd traveled from Kantinen, so unless we got very lucky, we'd probably be sleeping on the streets. Amelia, Night, and I were used to roughing it, of course, and I was sure Gilles and Crow would manage, but I worried about whether my classmates would be able to deal with that.

"Yup, works for me too!" Latticenail smiled, agreeing with Amelia. My theory was there wasn't actually a delay in the prize's arrival, but that they'd only prepared enough for one winner as they hadn't foreseen a tie. The bunnyman let out a heavy sigh of relief, but I couldn't shake the feeling there was a deeper reason for his unease.

Ever since we'd arrived on this continent, I'd felt plagued by a palpable sense of foreboding, and it always turned out to be warranted. First we got accosted by ruffians, then Amelia got kidnapped, then the monsters came flooding out of the labyrinth, then I almost died fighting the demons, then the hero's party showed up out of nowhere and convinced us to participate in this pageant, where we just so happened to meet the Demon Lord's daughter... It felt like we were hitting snags at every turn. At this point, I was confident that we got ourselves involved in more dangerous affairs on a daily basis than anyone else would in their lifetime. What had I done to be cursed with such awful luck?

"That about wraps it up, folks! Thank you all so much for coming out to this year's beauty pageant! We'll see you all next year back in Kantinen, in the beautiful Kingdom of Retice!"

I couldn't help but scoff. Retice was the country into which we'd originally been summoned, the one that had framed me for murder, and the one where more than half our classmates still remained. It was the largest of all human nations, so it made sense as a host country for the pageant. It also had a lot of beautiful greenery and pretty lakes, come to think of it. It was a very lovely place, in retrospect, though I could never see myself growing to love it while its current king and his daughter were still in power.

Suddenly, I felt the presence of someone standing in front of me, and I raised my head. I had a bad habit of getting lost in thought and losing sight of my surroundings. Thankfully, it was only Crow and Gilles.

"Hey, we need to talk. Come with us."

"Whoa, wait a sec!" I sputtered as the two men grabbed my hands and dragged me off into a dark alleyway. It was a rather seedy part of town, far removed from the gaudiness of the pageant. As soon as we made it far enough that we couldn't see the festival lights anymore, they unhanded me.

"What the hell did you drag me out here for?" I demanded in a huff, and the two of them looked at each other before answering.

"Truth is, we figured we'd end up having to stay the night in town, so we went out looking for inns preemptively," said Crow.

"And as we were doing so, we heard some rather unsettling rumors we thought you should be made aware of," added Gilles.

This gave me pause. *What kinds of rumors?* The use of the word *unsettling* led me to believe it was the kind of intel best discussed behind closed doors—the kind of intel that assassins and information brokers made their livings on. The kind of intel you had to stay abreast of if you wanted to make it in the underground sectors of society. Generally, such rumors were not to be taken lightly, even though new ones came out every day. One day, I'd need to learn the proper channels for keeping up to date on this sort of thing, but for now, I couldn't really call myself much of an assassin.

Crow nodded to indicate that he knew what I was thinking, then went on, "We stumbled across this information by pure chance, but apparently, a lot of people claim the winners of the competition each year turn up missing. And the average person has no clue this happens. It's apparently the main reason they have such a large number of contestants—so that, hopefully, no one will notice one or two going missing. But doesn't that still seem a little strange to you?"

"More than just a little," I said. "And it's not like people from society's dark underbelly don't interact with regular people, so if there's even a kernel of truth to these rumors, why haven't they spread like wildfire?"

"That, and it doesn't make sense that even someone like me hasn't heard of this before," said Crow. "Obviously, I've been retired for a long time, but I've always tried to keep my ear to the ground, and I have some pretty good sources... Which tells me this is something only a very small portion of underground societies might be privy to. Groups that work very hard to ensure information doesn't get leaked. And when it comes to shady dealings even *I* don't know about, there's only one big thing that comes to mind."

"And what's that?" I asked hesitantly.

He grimaced. "Human trafficking."

Human trafficking. It was among the worst crimes out there, even here in a brutal world like this. Back in Retice, when I'd had access to the castle archives, I'd read that long ago, the beastfolk used to sell the humans who came to their land in search of work into slavery, but the third hero to get summoned from my world put a stop to that.

There had only been four hero summonings before us, yet those four heroes had all left their mark on each of Morrigan's continents. Their stories were told in epic texts describing the heroic deeds of the first and second heroes and their work with the elves and demons long, long ago, as well as the work of the third and fourth heroes in more recent times that focused more on the humans and beastfolk.

The third hero was particularly famous for his work in martial arts, swordsmanship, and the abolishment of slavery. He taught the beastfolk, who were far more predisposed to physical combat than magic, the way of the sword and martial arts, and put a stop to the slave trade they'd been involved in. The hero himself, though human, was said to have been a giant bear of a man, with a bighearted personality that appealed to the beastfolk. He was said to be the most charismatic of all past heroes, and he was still a popular folk hero to this very day. Beastfolk mothers and fathers would use his example to teach their young that their powers should only ever be used to protect the weak, never to oppress them.

I looked over at Crow, only to see he was bearing his fangs and his fur was bristling up; he, like most beastfolk, despised even the idea of human trafficking. I recognized that Crow was genuinely unaware of this despicable part of beastfolk society, whether through willful avoidance of the topic or unintentionally. It was the sort of thing no one wanted to believe might still be happening right under their noses.

"And there's more to the rumors than that, actually. Some people think the whole thing about winners disappearing is just a sick joke someone's been spreading around to get their kicks, while other people think the contestants are being chopped up and spirited away, if you catch my drift. It's hard to find any concrete evidence of either theory, though, unfortunately."

I could only assume that by "chopped up," he was trying to imply that their organs were being sold on the black market.

I would have assumed these beautiful people were being sold alive as sex slaves or something, had I not already heard about the organ harvesting.

"Anyway, I just wanted you to be aware of what we heard. Especially since we're now well within you-know-who's territory, both physically and figuratively," Crow added, his eyes gloomy. He could only be referring to his sister's killer, the man known as Gram. Mali wasn't far from the city of Uruk, after which the country was named. If there really was human and organ trafficking going on here, there must have surely been someone working behind the scenes to keep the truth from leaking out. And with Gram's experience as ex-prime minister, that sort of secrecy seemed right up his alley. It was starting to seem more and more likely that he was involved.

"I'm trusting you to take care of what we talked about, Akira," Crow said, his dark eyes staring daggers right through me. It was the same look he'd had in his eyes that night in his workshop. It was enough to make my mouth immediately feel parched, and I recoiled a bit.

He was referring to what he'd requested of me back when I asked if he would come with us to the festival—the thing he said was the only reason he'd saved us from the demons. But I still hadn't given him a definitive answer, and it seemed he was getting a little impatient. For one thing, he almost never addressed me by name, so the fact that he was doing so now was probably an indicator of his seriousness. But it still wasn't the sort of thing I could decide on a whim, and I had no intention of letting him rush me to an answer. Crow realized I was indeed thinking it over and walked out of the alley, seemingly satisfied for now.

Gilles stayed back and looked down at me, his brow furrowed with concern. "Well, whatever it is, I can tell it's probably not the sort of thing I could offer any advice on. Just don't overexert yourself, and try not to pull your hair out over it, okay?"

Apparently, Crow hadn't told Gilles anything.

"Oh, right. Says the biggest workaholic and worrywart in all of Retice." I grinned. He seemed like a totally different person since leaving the castle, and I assumed the commander's death had a lot to do with that. But he'd still come all this way to track us down, and I could only assume he had a hand in helping the hero's party escape as well. It was almost like, despite his nervous temperament, he actively sought out and got himself wrapped up in as many precarious situations as he could find.

"I suppose you've got a point there," he said, wearing the most serious expression I'd ever seen.

When we left the alley, we ran into Amelia, Latticenail, and the hero's party, all gathered together in one big group. Amelia and Latticenail were chatting it up while the hero's party made a circle around them, watching from a distance.

"Oh! Akira, Crow wanted me to tell you he decided to head back to the inn," said Amelia.

Right, he did mention that they'd been out looking for a room, didn't he? I guess I got so caught up in the more repulsive topics we discussed that I forgot all about that part.

"Where were you planning to stay tonight, Latticenail?" I asked, since she was the outsider in the group.

She simply shook her head and rolled her eyes, casting a side-long glance over at the hero's party. "Eh, I'll prolly just find somewhere to camp out around here. Somethin' tells me your friends won't be able to sleep very soundly with little ol' me around!"

With that, Latticenail took her leave, and Amelia, who'd taken quite a shine to the little demon girl, began sulking.

"You really didn't want her to have to leave, did you?" I asked.

"I don't know what it is about her, but she reminds me of Kilika in a way. Makes me feel like I need to keep a close eye on her, y'know? Though if Kilika heard me saying that, she'd probably kill me."

I cocked my head quizzically. *Her and Kilika?* I had to admit, I couldn't really see the resemblance, but in fairness, I'd only interacted with the latter very briefly during a tense situation in the elven domain. I trusted that Amelia would know better than me, what with her being family and all.

"Well, I'm sure we'll run into her again tomorrow," I said, trying to reassure her.

If the rumors were true, then Latticenail was in the same amount of danger as Amelia, but judging by her stats, she was probably more prepared to handle an ambush than we were. Having her stay in the same inn as us would only make things easier for the criminals if they were to strike, and it's not like our group could offer Latticenail added protection, especially since there wasn't a lot of trust between her and my other classmates.

When we got to the inn, I was surprised to find it was a rather clean and fancy place. Beastfolk buildings had a reputation for the interiors not matching the exterior, so a nice-looking building would often end up being quite the pigsty inside, but the minimalistic monochrome interior of the inn was like that of a high-class hotel back in my world.

"Pretty nice place, I have to admit. But can we really afford it?" I asked Gilles quietly. Given we were a group made up mostly of hungry teenage boys, and Amelia had a bigger appetite than all of us combined, I was afraid we might not even be able to afford the room service bill—let alone the nightly fees—with just the money we had on hand. But Gilles simply smiled and told me not to worry about it, which puzzled me. Before I had time to think much more about it, though, a kind-looking beastfolk came out to greet us from the back room.

"Welcome to the Hotel Raven, everyone. My name is Corvo, and I'm the owner of this establishment. Please feel free to relax and make yourselves at home."

If the avian innkeeper of The Coop back in Ur had been a pigeon, then this fellow was a crow—though I didn't know enough about birds to say for sure. I was judging purely by the jet-black wings jutting out from his back. As he guided us to our room, Corvo attempted to make friendly conversation with us.

"I was an adventurer myself, you know, once upon a time. Your friend Crow actually saved my life back then, believe it or not. When I heard he and some friends of his were struggling to find accommodations for the evening, I sought him out and invited him to bring his party and stay here."

Ah, so that's how this panned out. There seemed to be an awful lot of people out there who owed Crow a favor or two, I'd noticed. The owner assured us there was no need to worry about the bill, and he guided us to one of the nicest rooms in the hotel—one that surely would have cost a fortune.

"Mr. Crow? Your friends have arrived," said Corvo, knocking on the door. Soon, Crow came to the door and opened it, letting us all see inside.

"Whoaaa!"

"Holy crap!"

My classmates oohed and aahed, and I simply stood there, dumbfounded.

"This is incredible!"

"Yeah, no kidding..."

The room was, like the rest of the hotel, monochrome in color, but the entire back wall was just one big window peering out over the festivities and the modest nightscape. *Guess we must be on the top floor, which explains why we had to climb all those stairs to get here.* What amazed me more than anything, though, was that the window didn't seem to be made of glass—it was clearly a sturdy wall just like the others, and yet we could see straight through it.

"That wall is made from translucent monster scales so our customers can enjoy the outside scenery to their hearts' content. Now then, please do let me know if there's anything else I can do for you all," Corvo said before taking his leave.

The room was all black and white, with the only hint of color being that of Crow, who was lounging on the black sofa and swirling a glass of wine in one hand, watching as the hero's party members filed in and marveled at the cityscape.

"Pretty nice room," I told him.

"Yeah, I honestly wasn't expecting to get something this nice for free... But Corvo ain't got ties to any shady underground dealings, and none of his employees are suspicious either. I think we can safely kick back and relax here." Apparently, Crow had done some digging on Corvo after hearing the unsavory rumors. He gulped down the contents of his glass, then made eye contact with me for the first time since we'd entered the room. "Anyway, I wouldn't worry too much about those rumors if I were you."

This was not the statement I had expected. Perhaps Crow was a more considerate person than I had originally thought, if he was trying to reassure me like this.

"Even though Amelia's the most likely target?"

"You're the type of guy who can jump into action from a state of relaxation in no time flat. You'd be better served to just treat things like business as usual than to get overly hung up on it. It's in her best interest too, trust me," Crow said as he gazed out the window once more.

I sighed, amused, before sitting down on the adjacent sofa. "Y'know, you almost sounded like a caring mentor just then."

"Didn't you hear? I used to take on apprentices, way back when... Though they always ended up getting sent to the hospital."

Amelia *had* mentioned this. Apparently, he'd been trying to pass on the secret technique taught to him by the Hero of Legend, but the process broke every pupil mentally and physically—that was the main reason he refused to teach Amelia.

"Y'know, I'm really curious—what *is* the secret technique, anyhow?" I asked.

Amelia hadn't told me what it actually did. I would have thought, given that Crow's class was blacksmith, any skill he could have possibly learned wouldn't be *too* hard for anyone else to pick up with a little motivation, but perhaps it had something to do with the ability he'd used to cancel out Mahiro's magic circles down in the labyrinth (not to mention the Shadow Magic controlling me) instantaneously.

Crow thought carefully for a while before answering. "To put it simply, it's an Extra Skill that can negate any and all types of magic. It's called Inversion. All you have to do is encounter a type of magic; then you'll be able to create an 'antimagic' that acts like a serum designed to perfectly counteract and negate that magic."

I was amazed. To think such a skill existed. No wonder Mahiro pulled back; without his magic circles, he was dead meat.

"But there *are* drawbacks to it. In order to use it, you need to learn the ancient tongue, and that's no mean feat when each and every rune is tinged with enough mana to make anyone go insane. If you fall in too deep while trying to learn it, you can and will lose your mind."

I assumed he was referring to the ancient runes lining the circumference of magic circles. I could see why they would be extremely difficult to learn, especially without the Understand Language Extra Skill, since they looked more like patterns than traditional characters.

"And even after you learn to read them, you still have to learn the vocabulary, which is a whole 'nother level of difficult... Took me nearly a hundred years to get it down."

Hang on. Didn't I hear that the average beastfolk lifespan was like, a hundred years and change? If it took him a hundred years to learn the ancient tongue, and that was before *he and the hero's party went and failed to slay the Demon Lord, which was already a hundred years ago... The math just doesn't add up.*

"How old are you anyway, Crow?" I asked.

"Who knows? It's not customary for beastfolk to ask one another's ages." He laughed, looking up and away from me. "I honestly couldn't tell you my exact age because I've forgotten it myself, but I've definitely been kicking around for at least two hundred years now."

I gawked. And nearly half that time was spent learning the ancient tongue? I couldn't imagine the kind of devotion and studiousness that would take. I could never stick to something for that long. Though I had to wonder: Why was he still alive?

"Well, actually, I remember the aging process started for me about fifty years after my sister was killed, so maybe I'm closer to two hundred and fifty or three hundred years old? Anyway, you can thank my whack job mother for the fact that I'm still around," he went on.

I had a hard time imagining anyone describing their mother

as a "whack job," especially when Crow was quite the eccentric himself. Maybe it was hereditary?

"I mean, what kind of lunatic drinks an immortality potion by accident? That's the only reason my mother is still alive and kicking, and it's her fault I've lived at least twice as long as your average beastman," he complained, before collapsing back into the sofa. Was he drunk? He seemed far more talkative and forthcoming than usual, and his current state reminded me of how the older guys I'd worked construction with had been when they got drunk.

"So you think her drinking an immortality potion is what gave you such a long life?" I asked, and he nodded, his eyes vacant.

"Yeah. That old crone drank the potion right before I was born, so it had a residual effect on me in the womb. It's all her damn fault."

I was pretty taken aback by his tone. It sounded like he resented her for something most people would be grateful to have. I could only conclude he longed for death, or at the very least he'd grown exhausted of living with only the search for revenge to keep him going. Japanese people had a longer average lifespan than people from other countries, but even among us, there weren't many who made it beyond a hundred years. Since I'd only been alive for a tenth as long as Crow, I couldn't even imagine what living so long would feel like. Maybe I could ask Amelia.

I noticed Crow had sunk down into the sofa cushions and fallen asleep. He looked very peaceful; it was not the expression of one who longed for death.

"I think it's probably best you let him sleep," said a voice from behind me.

I turned around to see Gilles standing there, a large comforter in his hands. I'd sensed him nearby a moment ago, and it was good to know my senses were still working properly. "How do you know Crow, anyway?" I asked as he covered Crow with the comforter.

He gave an awkward smile before sitting down on the white sofa across from me. "Well, you know he used to mentor pupils, correct?" he asked, and I nodded. We'd just been discussing that very subject. "One of those pupils was my mother. Though she's no longer with us, rest her soul."

My eyes widened a bit. Apparently, after Crow withdrew from the public eye, every country in Morrigan wanted to get their hands on the skill he'd acquired from the Hero of Legend, and they each sent representatives to try to learn it from him. Humans were no exception, and Crow did not refuse any apprentice at first; his desire for revenge was beginning to fade, and he was growing quite bored in his old age. Gilles's mother ended up losing her mind in pursuit of the skill, just like all the other apprentices.

"My father was an adventurer, and he died when I was still quite young, so my mother had to raise me all by her lonesome," Gilles went on. This reminded me of my mother, who was single, though she was too sickly to do much raising by the time my father left. "After her mental break, it was Crow who raised me. He was also the one who got me my position as a knight in the first place, and when he heard I'd left the force, he offered to take me in as a blacksmith's assistant while I searched for other work."

Gilles let out a wistful sigh as he looked lovingly down at the man sleeping on the couch. It was the same affectionate gaze one might expect a son to give their father, and a beautiful sight to behold.

"He's both a savior and a father figure to me. I don't hold what happened to my mother against him in the slightest. He's a bit of an oaf, I'll admit, but he's certainly not malicious."

"Yeah, so I've learned in the little time I've known him," I replied. "Anyway, what is it you're asking me to do with this information?"

I already knew Crow was a softie at heart who helped people in need. I wouldn't exactly call him a people person, but I could tell he was a good egg just from the way the owner of this hotel gushed about him. But why was Gilles regaling me with all these old stories?

"I was hoping you'd be willing to do what the old man asked of you. As you can probably surmise, he doesn't have much time left," said Gilles.

"I'd really prefer not to get myself mixed up in all of that."

I wasn't a charity worker, nor did I see myself as some champion of morality and righteousness. I did owe Crow my life, and I owed Gilles an awful lot for helping me escape the castle, but I still had my own main objective to fulfill. I needed to get home, and I knew the key to achieving that had to be somewhere in either the Demon Lord's castle or the castle of Retice. We'd been summoned here to slay the Demon Lord, but I'd noticed the magic circle they'd used to bring us here was almost identical to the ones the demon's second-in-command had used against us.

"Yes, I know you've got a lot on your plate as it is and that you're already anxious enough to head over to the Demon Lord's castle," said Gilles.

"Then would you please stop trying to—"

"It wouldn't even be much of a detour, I promise. Especially since you already swore to rescue and bring home the elves being held captive by his trafficking ring—or did you forget?"

I could have punched my past self in the face for that promise; I hadn't expected it to come back and bite me in the ass.

"Besides," Gilles continued, "you're going to need Crow to make it to the Demon Lord's castle anyway. I've never been there myself, but I've heard it's extremely easy to get lost along the way. And you certainly can't trust that demon girl to be your guide."

He had a point; having someone with experience traversing the hellscape of Volcano along for the journey *would* be a good idea. It wasn't as if we could just go out and buy a map of the continent, after all. We needed someone who was familiar with the lay of the land, so earning a favor from Crow might not be such a bad idea.

"You make a good point," I said. "But it's not such an easy thing for me to agree to, you understand."

I mean, what Crow asked me to do is something I'm morally opposed to on every level, I thought to myself as Gilles stood up and laid his hands on my shoulders.

"I've said my piece. The rest is up to you to decide. Though I would ask that you come to a decision quickly, because there's no telling how much time he has left."

After Gilles left the room, I simply sat there on the sofa, listening to Crow softly snoring as I gazed out upon the nightscape of the town glowing beautifully in spite of the moral quandary I was now being forced to confront.

"Have you been getting enough sleep lately, Akira?" Amelia asked me the next morning. She'd woken up before the others and seemed concerned upon discovering I'd already been up for quite some time, sipping my coffee-like beverage. The honest answer was no, I hadn't been sleeping much at all, and I knew exactly why. It was because of Crow's heavy request, and my conversation with Gilles the night before.

"No, not really, but it won't affect my combat ability, so don't worry. Besides, I could probably count on one hand the number of times I've gotten a full night's sleep in this world without literally fainting beforehand," I joked, raising a hand to cover part of my face. I probably looked like hell, and I should try to do something about it before the others woke up.

This only made Amelia more suspicious, however, and she moved my hand aside to get a good look at me, then cupped my face in both her hands. "You have a bad habit of trying to keep things to yourself, you know. Would it really kill you to rely on me a little bit more?" she asked.

"N-no, trust me, it's nothing you need to worry about..."

I sputtered, but I couldn't escape her discerning crimson eyes—especially not when she was holding my head in place. For the first time ever, I was afraid of those eyes.

"I understand you're probably only keeping quiet to protect us or someone else...but if that's how it's gonna be, then you leave me no choice but to take matters into my own hands. Because *someone's* got to look out for you," she said. I felt mana gathering around her, and my body became enveloped in a pale blue light. "Sorry to have to do this, Akira. Spellcraft... Forced Sleep!"

"Ame...lia..."

The last thing I saw before my consciousness faded was Amelia's face, looking down at me as though it pained her deeply to have to do this. It was then that I felt despair for having worried the one I loved enough that she felt she had no other choice but to force me asleep.

POV: AMELIA ROSEQUARTZ

AFTER DRAPING A BLANKET over Akira's limp body, I took a moment to examine his unconscious face. I traced my fingers along the dark circles beneath his eyes. They'd gotten a lot deeper, even since yesterday.

"Remind me never to get on your bad side, Princess," I heard a sleepy voice say. I looked up to see Crow staring at me from the sofa with a wide grin on his face.

I glared at him. "What did you say to Akira to make him like this?" I demanded, and Crow looked away before stretching his body like a cat. I simply stood there, shielding Akira without taking my eyes off of Crow.

"Hey, don't furrow those brows so much. You'll just get wrinkles prematurely. Besides, all I asked him for was a little reasonable compensation for saving his life."

I gasped as an image of him running to our rescue in the Great Labyrinth of Brute flashed through my mind. "Is that the only reason you came and saved us down there? Answer me," I demanded, glaring at him even harder.

At this suggestion, Crow grimaced ever so slightly. "Well, I dunno about that. I saved your sorry asses purely out of the goodness of my heart... It was only after the fact that I started thinking maybe I deserved a little thanks in exchange for my services. But I can see why you'd think that's lousy of me."

With this, his expression suddenly turned vulnerable, and I was a little disconcerted by it. I hadn't developed the same rapport with him as Akira had, so I still didn't understand what made the man tick. All I knew was that I'd rebuked him for acting like he'd given up on avenging his sister, then realized afterward he and I probably had a lot more in common than I'd initially thought. Now I wasn't sure if it was really fair for me to criticize him when I probably would have done the exact same thing.

"I used to look up to you an awful lot, y'know," he said, and I was about to scream at him for trying to change the subject when I realized what he'd just said, and my words caught in my throat. He looked at me, my mouth hanging open, and let out a chuckle. "I mean, you were the princess who saved the entire elven race in their hour of need, right? The little girl who used Resurrection Magic and Gravity Magic to save her people—almost sounds like something out of an epic poem or some legend. You were the type of person I always wanted to grow up to be...though my perceptions obviously changed once I actually met you and realized you're just as fallible as any other person."

"I hate people who put me on a pedestal like that," I replied. *Especially since it's usually followed by them looking down on Kilika like some sort of villain just because she was the one who accidentally caused that whole disaster.*

"Yeah, I'll bet," Crow said with a bitter smirk. "That's just the type of person you are... Anyway, did your boyfriend tell you I'm the one who made Lia's staff?" I shook my head. Akira and I hadn't had much time to sit down and talk lately, so there was probably a lot of information we had yet to exchange. "Well, it was the staff that let me know you guys were in peril. Speaking of Lia, did you notice her name is the last three letters of yours?"

"Are you implying that she was named after me?"

"That's right. I gave her that name because I wanted her to grow up to be a strong woman like you," he said.

I was genuinely a little surprised by this, though I quickly collected myself and squinted suspiciously at him. "And what exactly are you telling me this for?" I asked, unsure what Lia, a princess of Uruk, could possibly have to do with what we were talking about.

Crow scratched the back of his head and looked outside as the sun slowly rose over the city. "Not sure, really. I wanted to test this boy named Akira Oda you seem to admire so much and see if he's truly worthy to stand by your side, is all. When I named Lia after you, I thought there'd never be another person worthy of fighting alongside you, and I still feel that way."

My blood began to boil. "Do you have any idea how much unnecessary stress your selfish desires have piled on Akira?!" I snapped, and Crow froze. I couldn't see his expression amid the rising sun's glare through the window, but it felt like he was more vulnerable now than ever.

"I wasn't expecting him to stress about it so much. Though when I explained to him that the compensation I had in mind would also be in your best interest, he seemed conflicted. The boy loves you an awful lot, that's for sure, but not so much that he'd throw away his humanity for you."

Love could indeed make people blind. I'd lived far, far longer than Akira had, so I knew that much to be true. If Akira ever became too blind to tell right from wrong because of me, I would have no choice but to exit his life.

"He's every bit the man I thought he was." I smiled gently.

"So it would seem," said Crow, shrugging his shoulders and gazing into the sunrise. "But the fact he's conflicted at all means there's still a part of him that feels like he owes me. Something tells me all it would take for him to cast aside his humanity would be one last push... Like, say, if you were to be put in harm's way again."

In other words, *be careful.*

On that note, Crow shot a quick glance at Akira and then left the room. I never did get him to tell me what exactly he'd said to Akira, but what he did tell me was perhaps more astonishing.

"You...wouldn't throw away your humanity for me, would you, Akira?" I asked, knowing full well I wouldn't receive a reply.

POV: ASAHINA KYOUSUKE

WHEN I WOKE UP the next morning, I discovered Akira asleep on the couch and Princess Amelia sitting next to him, running her fingers through his hair. It had been quite a while since I'd last seen him asleep.

"It's quite rare to see him sleeping so vulnerably," I said, and Princess Amelia's shoulders shook a bit as she looked up at me. There was sadness in those eyes; something must have happened while I was asleep. But before I had the chance to ask, we were interrupted by Ueno, who had just woken up.

"What in the... Amelia, yer already awake?! Dang, I thought for sure I'd be the first!"

"Yeah. I couldn't sleep, really," said Amelia, still cradling Akira's head in her lap. The look in her eyes shifted closer to affection than melancholy.

"Hot dang! I ain't never seen Oda lookin' all defenseless like that... Well, nah, I guess I have, but it's sure been a hot minute!"

I nodded in agreement. Akira had a bit of a reputation for being the class's "sleeping beauty." He would stay awake for classes taught by teachers he was afraid of or who he knew would wake him up, but aside from that, he slept through the school day. It was a wonder he managed to avoid failing his exams, though I was probably the only person who knew that. If our other classmates caught wind of his grades, they probably would have accused him of cheating. Even I had been suspicious of him before I learned he often studied during spare moments at his many part-time jobs.

"Sounds like you know something about Akira I don't. Consider me curious," said Princess Amelia, and she and Ueno began chatting away, prompting me to take my leave ASAP.

"I'll be in the next room. Call me when you're ready to leave," I said.

"What the—?! Were you here the whole dang time, Asahina?!" shouted Ueno. Apparently, she genuinely hadn't noticed me. I thought she was simply ignoring me.

"Yes, I've been here all along," I said, before promptly exiting the room.

We were planning to go pick up the prizes for Princess Amelia, Latticenail, and Satou (who'd easily won the men's competition) later this afternoon. Apparently, the majority of entrants in the men's competition were big, bodybuilder types, so everyone who preferred simpler pretty-boys rallied their votes around Satou. Entering him in the men's pageant was always part of our plan, but we certainly hadn't expected him to actually win anything, so I did a double take when I heard he'd taken first prize.

We'd been doing a lot of thinking and digging over the past few days based on the intel Tsuda originally provided. The deeper we looked into it, the more likely it seemed our original suspect, the Uruk guildmaster, Gram, was involved in all of this. There was now little doubt he'd had a hand in the disappearances of the previous pageant winners, and he certainly wasn't doing much to hide it. Even without the use of a professional informant or investigator, we'd managed to gather all this information from regular adventurers like ourselves. In fact, it seemed that Crow and Gilles, who had been using private investigators, hadn't found enough pieces to confirm beyond a shadow of a doubt that Gram was involved. Now the question was whether we should tell Akira's group about our findings.

Upon exiting the room, I found Satou waiting for me, leaning against the wall. "Did you find the answer you were looking for?" he asked, and I nodded.

The dark circles under Akira's eyes were growing deeper with each passing day, which was why I'd fought back when Satou and the others insisted we should tell Akira everything we knew. Obviously, the safest thing to do would be to tell everyone to tighten security around Princess Amelia and Satou in anticipation of an ambush. But after seeing Akira just now, I'd only grown more steadfast in my resolve.

"I still don't think we can tell Akira... Though knowing him, he's begun doing some investigating of his own by now," I said.

"Such as?"

"Haven't you noticed? Night's been missing ever since yesterday evening. Whether he's standing guard somewhere to protect Princess Amelia or out gathering intel on his own, I couldn't tell you, but the fact that he's Akira's familiar means that he can communicate and act on Akira's orders even from afar."

Though opting not to share our intel with Akira would require that we come up with some sort of excuse as to why we hadn't told him sooner.

But it seemed Satou was convinced, as he nodded. "Well, you know Akira better than the rest of us. So I say we should trust your judgment on this."

I smiled weakly. Satou had known Akira just as long as I had. How sad it was that our relationships with him were so different. "Let's let Ueno keep Amelia preoccupied while the rest of us go over the plan one last time. Gram's sure to go after the pageant winners before long, but it's possible we can use me as a decoy, since I'm technically a winner too. C'mon, the others are waiting back in the bedroom."

I voiced my agreement and followed him back to our private quarters. I hadn't seen Akira sleeping as soundly as he had been in quite some time. The past several days, he'd been going to sleep after us and waking up before us. I wasn't sure if he was getting less sleep than he normally would or if he wasn't able to sleep at all, but it was clear just from looking at him that his health was taking a hit as a result. Maybe having Princess Amelia next to him was what allowed him to sleep peacefully again. Regardless of why, it was good to see him getting sufficient rest while he could. I'd noticed Akira seemed to have become a more laid-back person since he met Amelia. Though I was worried that if anything ever happened to her, he'd turn into a killing machine in an instant.

POV: AMELIA ROSEQUARTZ

"HEY, YOU SURE it was a good idea to leave him snoozin' in there?" Crow asked me once we were on our way to collect the prizes at the location they'd given us yesterday. Akira had still been asleep by the time we were heading out, so we just left him lying on the sofa. Crow had already returned to his normal, brusque manner of speaking, despite talking more softly and politely with me earlier this morning. He'd even made it sound like he knew all about me and Kilika.

The news about monsters from the Great Forest Labyrinth flooding out and massacring the elves was big news at the time, and it quickly reached the shores of the other continents; sharing information regarding demon and monster attacks was also required by law in order to prepare for any potential demon invasions. It was commonly known by people at the time that Kilika had caused the incident by placing too much bait at the labyrinth's entrance because that was what the official reports had stated. However, no reports of the incident remained after my father had all documents destroyed, so the only feasible way one could know the specific details (especially about Kilika) would be if they were alive at the time. Based on the beastfolk lifespan, there was no way Crow had been alive that long. I wanted to ask him about it, but if by some chance I'd misinterpreted his reaction and I ended up revealing Kilika's secret after everyone worked so hard to sweep it under the rug, I'd feel terrible, so I refrained from broaching the subject.

"Akira's been overexerting himself a lot lately, so he needs his rest. Besides, we're just going to pick up the prizes and then head straight back to the inn. It'll be fine," I said. Once we had our prizes, we had no need to stay in Mali any longer. We could head out as soon as Akira woke up—he might even be awake by the time we got back.

"Gotcha... Well, here's hoping we all make it out of here alive, I guess," Crow mumbled, though I wasn't able to catch the last few words he said.

"Welp, this is the place... Er, ain't it?" asked the Ueno girl, whose confidence faded upon seeing the dingy, dilapidated building in front of us. It was an old hotel—certainly not the sort of place one would expect to pick up any grand prizes. All at once, the mood of the entire group tensed up. We'd been on high alert today from the start, but I didn't think anyone could have foreseen this turn of events.

"Wha... Who's there?!" shouted Crow. I whirled around to see a single man, dressed in black, standing behind us. The others quickly turned their gazes on him as well.

"You're...that committee representative, right? Lapin, was it?" the Hosoyama girl asked, her eyes wide. She was right; at first, I thought it might have just been long white hair, but they were definitely the floppy bunny ears of the man we'd met yesterday. Only this time, he didn't seem at all meek and cowardly, but instead stood before us fully confident, almost foreboding.

"Looks like it's you they're after, princess," said Crow.

I snapped back to my senses and saw that several other men, also dressed in black, had begun to surround us. They seemed rather unintimidated by the fact that we had both the current hero's party and a member of the previous one with us, not to mention my own combat prowess. There were about twelve of them in all, and they quickly closed in on us, leaving no room to escape.

"You're the real Princess Amelia, I take it?" said one of the men.

Immediately, the hero's party members formed a circle around me to protect me from their advance. They reacted so quickly, it was almost as if they'd been expecting an ambush. But now wasn't really the time to be concerned about that.

"Yes, and what business is it of yours?" I said, narrowing my eyes. The men in black looked at each other and nodded. Even without a skill like Detect Danger, I could tell these men weren't looking for a simple chat.

"Lord Gram would like to speak with you. You'll be coming with us now."

I felt Crow go into ferocious mode beside me. Gram was, after all, the name of his sister's killer.

"And why, pray tell, should the princess of the elves deign to answer the summons of a mere guildmaster?"

It was supposed to be the royals who did the summoning, not the other way around. The disregard for common etiquette was disrespectful to say the least. Yet my words were lost on the men in black, as they simply stepped closer. They were determined to take me by force if they had to. Behind them, I could hear Lapin cackling maniacally.

"Oh, Princess. What were you thinking, coming to a place like this with only a bunch of kids and an old man past his prime to protect you? Why, you didn't even bring that boy who's always following you around," the bunnyman taunted.

Apparently, it had been Akira they were most worried about...
Perhaps they didn't know these were members of the hero's party.
They needed to take a page out of Akira's book and do their
research beforehand. I let out a heavy sigh, then held one hand
out in front of me.

"Gravity!"

Immediately, the men in black all fell to their knees under
the sheer weight of my magic. I used to have a hard time controlling it so that it only affected my enemies and not my allies,
but I'd learned how to better direct it during my time with
Akira down in the labyrinth. I was feeling a little weary since I'd
just created a new spell with Spellcraft, which drained a fair bit
of my MP, but I still had more than enough to deal with these
ruffians.

"And where exactly was it you were planning to take me, hm?"
I asked, looking down at the men now trembling on all fours.
I probably looked quite cold and terrifying in that moment; it
wasn't a side of me I ever wanted Akira to see, but if I had to resort
to torture to get an answer out of them, I was absolutely prepared
to do that. I wasn't raised like your average pampered princess,
after all. The high elf nobility had ruled over the Sacred Forest for
hundreds and hundreds of years, and our people had been forced
to do many unsavory things to protect that rule. I was not the
sweet, beautiful woman Akira thought I was. I might have acted
like a carefree, absentminded fool around him, but you could be
sure I would not sit idly by whenever some terrible villain made
an attempt on my life.

"If you don't feel like answering the question, I'll be happy to squash you all like bugs," I said, lowering my hand just a bit. Even this was enough added force to make their bones audibly crack, and they all collapsed down on the ground.

POV: SATOU TSUKASA

I<small>T ALL HAPPENED</small> so fast. One minute, we were suddenly surrounded by a bunch of strange men in black clothes, and the next, they'd all been brought to their knees. All we did to help was stand around and watch. We might as well have not been there at all.

"Now, answer me. What are you people after? Where is Gram, and what is he plotting?" demanded Amelia as she lowered her hand to amplify the force again. Her eyes were cold and full of hatred, almost to the point that I myself felt pressured to answer her question myself. My other party members were starting to look rather pale from fright as well.

We'd all sort of assumed Amelia was a weak fighter. We'd never seen her fight before, so we had no way of envisioning how she might handle herself in combat. Our whole plan had been developed around the idea that she couldn't protect herself, so it had been misguided from the very beginning. I had to wonder if Akira knew things would play out like this, and that was why he'd been so lackadaisical.

"W-we don't know anything! H-honest!" blathered the committee representative, fear painted all over his face. But Amelia was not moved by the man's pitiful plea; if anything, she seemed offended by it.

"Do you know what I hate more than anything else in this world?" she asked, lowering her slender arms even further. There was no longer even a flicker of light in her eyes; to the screaming men floundering on the ground, they probably looked like the eyes of death. "I'll give you a hint: it's being lied to. And I don't believe for a second you don't know anything. I've lived hundreds of years longer than you fools. You really think you can pull a fast one on me?"

The fact that elves lived extremely long lives was such common knowledge in this world that even our group knew it, despite never getting an education about this world back in Retice. Though I never knew they could be such ferocious fighters too. Eventually, Crow stepped up and gave the silent men a harrowing warning.

"I'd answer the lady's question if I were you. She's dead serious."

In other words, she was more than ready to commit murder. And this world wasn't like Japan; if she felt sufficiently threatened by these men, then we had no right to stop her from doing so in self-defense. Not that we *could* stop her even if we tried—all we could do was watch from the sidelines as the men were squashed into pancakes.

"A-all right, all right! W-we'll talk!" screamed one of the men as his bones began to snap under the pressure. A few seconds later, and it would have been too late.

Amelia raised her arms up a bit, but she did not stop casting her spell completely. "Then you can explain yourselves from down there. Try anything funny, and I'll crush you all."

As Amelia stared them down, one of the men in black began to explain how they sold the pageant winners' organs on the black market. All of what he said perfectly aligned with the intel Tsuda had brought to our attention initially, and it sounded like Amelia had indeed been their target this time around. Her expression gradually grew more and more grim.

"I see," she said. "So there never was any grand prize, and your plan all along was to dismember me and sell off my parts to depraved lunatics, then." Whether intentionally or not, she began to slowly lower her casting hand once more. But just before the men were crushed completely, someone jumped out from the shadows and accosted her—someone I recognized, but not necessarily someone I trusted.

"Okay, I think that's enough!" said the girl. "Sheesh, Princess! You can't just go doin' stuff like that! This isn't the Sacred Forest, y'know. You can't just execute people on the spot, even if they *are* lowlife scum!"

It was Latticenail—the demon who'd tied with Amelia to win first prize in the pageant. I was busy participating in the men's competition, so I hadn't witnessed the action myself, but even from the men's stage, we had heard the uproarious cheering when she walked out on stage.

"Why, hello, Latty," said Amelia. "Last I checked, citizens *do* have the right to execute criminals who have wronged them in this country. Granted, it usually requires an officially sanctioned duel to the death, but these men all came at me with the intention to kill, and I merely defended myself. I think a judge would probably find that this counts as a fair substitute for a duel."

That was an awfully unsettling thing to hear Amelia say, especially since her face was devoid of expression. Still, the demon girl refused to let go of her hand.

"If you ask me, even the baddest of bad guys has his own story to tell, and no other person has the right to take the chance away from him. So please, don't go killing other people when I'm around, okay?" said the demon. There was calmness in her purple eyes peeking out from beneath her hood, yet firmness in her tone. The sudden change in her behavior seemed to surprise Amelia so much so that her hand went limp, ending her spell. Finally, the demon let go of Amelia's wrist, and put on her carefree smile once more.

"But I mean, if you *really* wanna kill 'em, feel free to do it when I'm not looking, I guess! I may be a defender of the law with a strict moral code, but that doesn't mean I can protect *everyone*, now, does it? I can't be everywhere, and sometimes accidents happen!"

The men, who had been scrambling to try to escape, were now frozen in place, paralyzed in fear by the impish demon girl's frightening indifference.

As Crow handed the men in black off to the authorities, I couldn't help but think to myself: What had we even come here for? Obviously, we were hoping to expose Gram's evil deeds and gain Akira's favor, but in the end, we hadn't really accomplished anything. All we had done was invite Akira to the festival, enter the contest, and win as a decoy we didn't need, and try to act as bodyguards for someone who didn't need protecting. Hell, I wasn't even sure I had the power to protect *anyone* at this point. In fact, I was feeling more powerless now than I'd ever felt in my life.

POV: ODA AKIRA

IT FELT ALMOST LIKE I was slowly sinking further and further into a deep, dark ocean, swaying in the gentle currents as they carried me down to its deepest fathoms.

"Where am I...?"

I was surprised to find I could still speak as my voice reverberated through the darkness, but I still had no control over my body. I struggled to recall the last thing that happened to me before ending up here.

"Right, Amelia put me to sleep..."

That was it. She crafted a new spell and induced a Forced Sleep in me, probably out of concern for the growing dark circles beneath my eyes. When I remembered the look on her face right before she cast it on me, I let out a heavy sigh. It was my fault for pushing myself so hard despite my lack of sleep. I'd need to apologize to her after I woke up.

After calming down a bit, I tried to assess my current predicament. Considering Amelia had used Forced Sleep, and I had no recollection of waking up, I could only assume that I was still asleep and in some sort of dream state at the moment. Maybe

I could try using World Eyes and see what information showed up? Though since my eyes were closed, I didn't have particularly high hopes.

"Yeah, no dice."

I couldn't use World Eyes, or any of my skills for that matter. It was just a dream, after all. So now what was I supposed to do? But before long, I felt something press up against my back. Sticking with the metaphor that I was sinking down into a deep, dark ocean, then this would have been the ocean floor, yet it felt far too flat and warm. But since I couldn't move my body, all I could do was lie there and listen to a distant voice.

"If you don't feel like answering the question, I'll be happy to squash you all like bugs."

It was so soft that it was drowned out by the sound of my breathing, but I could never mistake this voice—it was Amelia, though her tone was uncharacteristically cold. I could tell it wasn't a friendly conversation. It was the first time I'd ever heard such animosity in her voice—even when I first rescued her and she wasn't sure I could be trusted, I never felt any malice from her. She was, understandably, very cautious around me at first, presumably because she'd checked my stats with World Eyes, but she never treated me like I was nothing.

"Do you know what I hate more than anything else in this world? I'll give you a hint: it's being lied to. And I don't believe for a second that you don't know anything. I've lived hundreds of years longer than you fools. You really think you can pull a fast one on me?"

To be fair, I could see how someone might mistake Amelia

for a girl around my age, even if they knew about elven lifespans. Even I sometimes forgot she was actually hundreds of years older than me, like when she was chatting it up and giggling with my female classmates.

"I'd answer the lady's question if I were you. She's dead serious."

This time, it was Crow's voice, and it was even fainter than Amelia's. From the context of the discussion, it sounded like this was happening on the way to pick up the prizes from the pageant, which told me the rumors Crow and Gilles had told me about were true. After Crow's warning, I heard a third voice crying frantically about something, but it was too indistinct for me to make out. Apparently, I could only pick up the voices that were closest in proximity to Amelia. Maybe this was an unintended side effect of her new spell, and the mana had forged a link between us while I was under her spell.

"Then you can explain yourselves from down there. Try anything funny, and I'll crush you all."

I couldn't help but grimace at the merciless tone of Amelia's voice. Just then, I felt a wave ripple through the ocean-like space I was suspended in, almost like the water level was being lowered... Was I trapped in a metaphorical basin of Amelia's mana reserves and feeling the effects of her using some of it? It would certainly make sense that it felt like an ocean, if that was the case, since her mana supply was nearly infinite. Maybe I could ask Crow about it after I'd woken up. If my theory was correct, then the level had lowered because she'd just cast a spell—probably Gravity Magic, judging from the "I'll crush you all" line.

"And your plan all along was to dismember me and then sell my parts to some depraved lunatics, then."

I could almost taste the venom in her words, though I had a hard time believing she had any intention of actually killing these goons. I was disappointed in myself for being unable to go to her aid, but then, I had to strain my ears and listen as an unintended challenger joined the fray.

"Okay, I think that's enough!"

The sound of Latticenail's peppy, rambunctious voice set my mind at ease. Maybe she had come to collect her grand prize as well. It was odd how relieved I felt to have her on the scene, considering we'd only just met yesterday, and she was a demon to boot.

"Sheesh, Princess! You can't just go doin' stuff like that! This isn't the Sacred Forest, y'know. You can't just execute people on the spot, even if they are *lowlife scum!"*

She must have closed the distance between her and Amelia, because I could now make out her voice far more clearly than Crow's. *Also, since when do demons have a problem with wanton killing?* I listened to Amelia argue with her. Personally, I didn't see any reason she had to kill these guys, even if they *were* criminals. Then, as if speaking my own words by proxy, Latticenail expressed the same sentiment to Amelia in an uncharacteristically solemn voice.

"If you ask me, even the baddest of bad guys has his own story to tell, and no other person has the right to take the chance away from him. So please, don't go killing other people when I'm around, okay?"

I was beginning to doubt this girl was truly a demon at all. At this point, I wouldn't be surprised if there was some massive twist where she turned out to be a past hero, even. Hell, I'd welcome her to the team without a second thought.

"But I mean, if you REALLY wanna kill 'em, feel free to do it when I'm not looking, I guess! I may be a defender of the law with a strict moral code, but that doesn't mean I can protect everyone, now, does it? I can't be everywhere, and sometimes accidents happen!"

Welp, there went that theory. How very like her to almost say something inspiring and then spoil it at the last minute. Not long after, I suddenly felt my consciousness rising rapidly to the surface, and it seemed Amelia's spell was about to wear off. When I finally regained control of my body and shot awake, it felt like coming up to the surface after a deep dive, gasping for air.

My Status as an
Assassin Obviously
Exceeds the Hero's

✦ CHAPTER 3 ✦

Uruk, City of Water

POV: AMELIA ROSEQUARTZ

"WELCOME BACK."

When we returned to our room at the Hotel Raven, we were greeted by a very awake and very alert Akira. I was relieved to see he was looking a lot better by all accounts—even the bags under his eyes were gone.

"Good to be back," said Crow, who was the first into the room, as he put his tired feet up. Akira didn't ask me anything or even shoot me a dirty look.

"Once you all have a chance to rest, gather up your things so we can leave town ASAP. Crow, Gilles, Amelia, Mr. Hero, and Kyousuke, meet me over in the next room," Akira said.

"Roger."

Everyone jumped into action in response to Akira's directions. It felt like he was begrudgingly taking a leadership role since Crow seemed utterly uninterested in doing so. We all gathered in the other room as Akira had instructed, naturally arranging ourselves into a circle.

"Okay, it's time to decide our next course of action," he began. Immediately, the hero and Kyousuke cocked their heads in confusion, and Akira scratched the back of his neck and looked away, which I recognized as something he only did when he was embarrassed. Akira had previously denied the hero's party the right to travel alongside us, yet the fact that he had called them to discuss our next move could only mean one thing.

The hero looked both overjoyed and bewildered by this turn of events, and he was the first to respond. "Whoa, whoa, whoa. I mean, I'm glad you're letting us tag along, but why the sudden change of heart?"

"I know all about how guys have been going around trying to investigate Gram's little organ harvesting business. I never asked you to prove to me you've got what it takes. All I said is that we don't need any dead weight members who can't protect themselves. And in the end, you guys proved you knew how to assess the situation and take preemptive action to protect someone other than yourselves... That's more than good enough for me. I can't say I'm thrilled you got in so far over your head without telling me about it, but I'll let it slide this time. I know it couldn't have been easy."

Kyousuke and the hero both let out heavy sighs of relief. Apparently, they'd both been worried about what Akira might do when he found out they'd kept this from him.

"Anyway," Akira continued, "it's time to decide our next move.

We have two options: we either dive headfirst into demon terri-tory in search of the Demon Lord, or we take a quick detour over to the capital city of Uruk, where we'll most likely find Gram."

The hero clearly wanted the former, while Crow obviously preferred the latter; both were places we'd need to go eventually. We'd succeeded in handing Lapin over to the authorities, but he was just a lowly pawn. Actually getting to Gram would probably be a much more difficult endeavor.

"Which one are you leaning toward?" asked Crow. "Not in-cluding any outside factors that might sway you one way or the other."

I wasn't sure what "outside factors" Crow was referring to, but he stared deeply into Akira's eyes as Akira contemplated his answer.

"Well, from everything I've heard about Volcano, it sounds like a place that's very complicated to get around in, and with few safe havens in which we could hide. To make matters worse, Night tells me that ever since his little battle with Mahiro down in the Great Labyrinth of Brute, he's had any information related to the demon continent and its layout wiped from his brain."

Almost reflexively, I looked at Akira's shoulders, where Night was usually perched, yet found them empty, as they had been empty for the past few days. I knew there had to be a reason Night was gone, but Akira didn't seem at all concerned about it, so I held my tongue.

"As such," Akira continued, "I think we'll need the help of a bona fide expert before we even attempt to tackle the demon continent. Someone who's directly familiar with all of its ins and outs…even if that knowledge might be more than a century out of date."

All eyes in the room immediately turned to Crow. If anyone knew how to traverse through demon territory, it would be the guy who'd made it all the way to the Demon Lord's castle and lived to tell the tale. The legends said he and the previous generation's hero party had spent close to fifty years investigating the land of Volcano before finally reaching it.

"It's true; you might even say that Volcano's something like a summer home for me…and I guarantee it hasn't changed much over the past hundred years," Crow said.

"Erm, do you have any basis for that assumption, or…?" the hero asked, and Crow glared at him.

"Sure I do. It's very simple: the demons don't feel threatened by us in the slightest. Maybe the foul monsters prowling their lands do, but not the demons themselves. They know they're stronger than any of the other races, so they feel no need to build up their defenses or even exercise the most basic amount of caution. No way has that changed in the last hundred years."

Come to think of it, I remembered Night telling us there were demons who went their entire lives without ever experiencing pain, and that, while they were obviously most well-known for their overabundance of mana, their vitality, strength, and defense were also far greater than any of the other races. The kinds of tiny scratches and scrapes one might suffer just from little everyday accidents didn't even register to them, and they didn't usually get wounded in combat either. Thinking back on it now, it really was a miracle that we'd made it out of the labyrinth alive.

"In other words, we'll need Crow's help if we want to have any hope of making it to the Demon Lord," said Akira. "And he tells me he'd be happy to serve as our guide, so long as I help him with another favor beforehand. And in order to do that, I'll need to go to Uruk first."

What could this "favor" be? I don't like the sound of it at all.

"So my plan was to go to Uruk first, then head over to Volcano. But we could also split into two teams, if that's what the group would prefer, because I can certainly take care of this little favor for Crow on my own."

A favor that Akira can take care of alone... Honestly, what could it possibly be?

"Obviously, my personal preference, barring all outside factors, would be to dash straight over to the Demon Lord's castle so we can all go home... But sometimes there's a necessary order of events in order to ensure the greatest likelihood of success."

So we would be making a quick stop in the city of Uruk before heading to the demon continent, then. I didn't mind the detours, since I would go wherever Akira went, but it seemed the two members of the hero's party were far more conflicted about this decision.

"What about the demon girl we met yesterday? You seemed to get on well with her. Couldn't we just ask her to be our guide?" asked Kyousuke.

It was true Latty was a demon, and far more good-natured than one might expect a demon to be—judging by what happened earlier, she even seemed to have a strong sense of justice, which put her in stark contrast to demons like Mahiro. It was entirely possible she'd agree to help us out if we asked, but there was one little detail that made asking her a bad idea all around.

"And here I thought you guys wanted nothing to do with Latticenail... Regardless, I'm afraid that's not gonna work," Akira replied.

Something told me they were only suggesting her as an option so that they wouldn't need to make the detour to attain Crow's help. I made eye contact with Akira and nodded to indicate I would take it from here.

"We did consider that option, of course," I began. "But the way Latty tells it, she's hardly ever set foot outside of the Demon Lord's castle, so she isn't very familiar with the continent."

Akira had instructed me to ask Latty if she'd be willing to be our guide through the demon continent, and I'd finally had a chance to ask her earlier today. I simply stated that we had business at the Demon Lord's castle and asked if she'd be able to guide us there. She'd smiled and shook her head.

"Nah, I'm kind of a sheltered child, actually. Born and raised in the castle and never set a foot outside the darn thing, or even seen the land I was supposed to rule! Kinda the whole reason I ran away from home, actually..."

"Then how did you ever manage to make it all the way here?"

"Oh, it wasn't all that tough... I just flew right on over!"

"Pardon...?"

I had no idea what she meant, but I knew better than to call Latty a liar. So it was safe to assume she had no experience actually traversing the continent and thus wouldn't be of much help to us. Upon hearing all of this, the two dissenters from the hero's party finally relented.

"So what *is* this favor, anyway?" asked the hero, and Akira immediately clammed up. Crow, meanwhile, was looking off in a totally different direction, clearly not listening to the conversation.

"Yeah, uh... About that..."

Akira's eyes were wandering, and I could clearly tell that he was fumbling to come up with some sort of excuse. He had no intention of telling us the true favor.

"I just need to help Crow out with a little something. Something an old grandpa like him can't do by himself anymore. Hence why I said we don't need to bring the whole gang...in fact, I'd almost prefer to just handle it myself."

I cast a sidelong glance at Crow, who seemed happy with this explanation, so maybe it wasn't technically a lie. However, Akira was clearly neglecting to address the true heart of the matter for a reason.

"Gotcha. In that case, maybe the rest of us really ought to go on ahead. We'll just need to pick someplace to meet back up again after you're done. Know anywhere that might be good?" asked the hero.

"Why not somewhere in this area?" posited Gilles, unraveling a map and pointing to a specific part. "We would be within striking distance of demon territory while still remaining safe within the beastfolk domain."

As I half-listened to their deliberations, I peered into Akira's eyes and saw the hesitation lurking deep within. It seemed my Forced Sleep spell had only healed his physical weariness and had done nothing to solve whatever was gnawing at his brain. I could only assume this favor Crow had asked of him was the underlying cause for his recent lack of sleep.

"No way. Not there," Crow butted in, outright vetoing the location on the map Gilles had suggested.

"Why not? It's the nearest point on the continent to Volcano, and as such we could easily launch our offensive whenever we so desired," Gilles argued.

Crow let out a sigh of frustration. "'Cause that's where..." Crow grumbled, trailing off.

"Come again?"

"'Cause that's where the old bag lives, and I don't wanna go anywhere near it! Don't make me say it again!" Crow snapped impatiently.

For a moment, I assumed "the old bag" might be referring to his grandmother or something, but then Akira provided some much-needed context.

"He's talking about his mom, for the record," he whispered in my ear.

I nodded, but as the information sank in, a thought occurred to me: If Crow was already approaching the end of his own lifespan, then how in the world was his *mother* still alive? But when I turned to Akira for an explanation, I found that he was smiling sheepishly at Crow, apparently realizing he'd already said too much.

"Besides, there's an old abandoned shack just a little bit west of there. My old party used it as a safe house back in the day, so there should still be plenty of supplies stockpiled inside," Crow said, and I gasped. I had heard rumors of the various safe houses the previous hero's party had used during their time preparing to attack the Demon Lord.

"Then it sounds like we've got our rendezvous point," Akira said.

With that, our next course of action was decided. The mysteries surrounding Crow were only growing deeper and deeper, yet I held out hope that maybe this next leg of our journey wouldn't be quite so perilous as the last few.

POV: ODA AKIRA

"OKAY, see you guys later."

"Don't go dying on us out there, Akira!"

"Yeah, same to you."

The conversations with the rest of the team went relatively smoothly, and soon it was time for us to leave. Gilles and the hero's party would be leaving first, heading straight for the previous hero party's safe house at the northernmost tip of Brute. The rest of us would be going with Crow to the city of Uruk, which Gram called home. With Gilles's magic, the hero's party would be leaving little markers as they went that were imperceptible to the average person, almost like a trail of breadcrumbs.

The area where the safe house was located was apparently quite dangerous and filled with many ferocious beasts and monsters, and it was infamous for being a place where even high-ranking adventurers often met their end. In a certain sense, their group had a far more dangerous path ahead of them than mine did. While I was sure Gilles would do everything he could to keep them safe, and the hero and Kyousuke were certainly strong enough to hold their own, I was definitely worried about the girls and animal trainer surviving the trek. So when Nanase and the others joked about me not dying on them, I could only smile awkwardly in response.

"Until we meet again. Be safe out there," said Kyousuke.

"Just so you know, you guys are probably the ones with the more arduous quest ahead of you," I said, and he simply nodded like the dutiful samurai he was.

"I'm well aware. But I'm sure yours will be dangerous too. There aren't many things in this world that would cause you to hesitate."

My words caught in my throat. Sometimes Kyousuke really did know how to cut straight to the heart of the matter. He always had, even back in our world, but it had taken the form of an Intuition skill here. Now it felt like he was more perceptive than ever.

"Right. I'll be careful." I tried my best to flash a reassuring smile, but Kyousuke clearly wasn't buying it. He simply went to join the rest of the hero's party.

"What, you didn't tell him?" asked Crow, who had snuck up beside me without me noticing. I wasn't sure what he was expecting; it wasn't exactly the sort of thing one could just mention off the cuff.

"Of course not. And if I was gonna tell anyone, it would be Amelia," I replied, and Crow simply rolled his eyes with a wry smirk before walking over to Gilles. *Hey, buddy. You're the one who asked. Don't gotta be snarky about it.*

"Time for us to get going, Akira."

"Yeah, okay. See you guys later," I said, waving goodbye to my fellow classmates, knowing I might not see them again.

"Later, Akira."

"Yep. Later." I turned my back and refocused myself on the task at hand. After all, even if they were successful in their quest, it wouldn't mean a thing if we couldn't pull off ours... I needed to mentally prepare myself to do what I had to do.

"Do you know anything about the city of Uruk, Akira?" asked Amelia, her face shrouded by a hood as we walked toward our destination. The road from Mali to Uruk had not been well-maintained, and it was more like an overgrown forest trail. Crow brought up the rear, following the rest of us at a slight distance.

"Nope, not a thing," I replied. "Just that it's the grandest city in all of Brute."

"Yep. It's by far the biggest, and the wealthiest. There's all sorts of delicious foods to try too!" She beamed, and I chuckled. I could only assume that was the part *she* was most looking forward to.

At our current pace, we were likely to reach the city in a week or two; times like these made me really miss cars. Hell, I would have even settled for a horse-drawn carriage or a wagon.

"Uruk is known as the City of Water," Crow informed us. "There are several rivers that crisscross through town, so it's primarily connected by canals instead of roads, and most transit is done by boat. It's a very pretty town, and the rise in tourism is probably what's led to it becoming such a major city in recent years."

"Y'know, that sounds an awful lot like a city somewhere in my world."

"Does it?"

I nodded, trying to conjure up the image from one of my social studies textbooks, which had been burned into my memory. Venice, I think the place was called. I would have loved to go check it out, but international vacations were kind of a pipe dream for my family, especially given my mom's condition.

"I'll take care of finding us an inn, so you guys can just go do some sightseeing," Crow muttered under his breath, and Amelia and I looked at each other. Was Crow actually trying to be considerate? It was kind of cute.

"Uruk's where Lia lives too, isn't it? We could meet up with her."

"Yeah, I contacted her as we were leaving the hotel. Said she'll be happy to give us a guided tour around town assuming her schedule doesn't fill up."

At this, I cocked my head. The way Crow was talking today didn't seem like him at all. He was being so...thoughtful.

"...What? If you've got something to say, then say it," he grumbled, and I was honestly a little relieved to see him transform back into his usual grumpy self. *Yes, that's the Crow we know and love.*

"Sorry, I've just never seen you act like this before, so I was a little thrown off," I said, and Crow went quiet. But then he thrust his head up to the sky.

"I treat people with the level of respect I think they deserve. If I see potential in someone, they get to know the real me. Those little herolings had no potential, but you guys do. That's all there is to it," he said, in a very succinct and Crow-like manner.

"So does that mean you'll teach me the Hero of Legend's secret technique now?" asked Amelia. I was amazed she hadn't given up on that by now. In fact, I was pretty sure she had, as she wasn't bowing her head and groveling at his feet anymore, begging him to teach her every day.

"If that's really what you want, we can give it a shot. But I won't be held accountable for anything that might happen to you as a result," said Crow with a sigh of resignation, and Amelia looked like she wanted to let out a cheer.

Exactly two weeks after we parted ways with the hero's party, we arrived in Uruk, capital city of the nation that bore the same name. We were running just a little bit behind schedule due to the many breaks we took along the way so Crow could teach Amelia the fundamentals of the first hero's legendary Extra Skill, Inversion.

The runes and everything he taught her were extremely difficult to follow, even for a guy like me with the Understand Language Extra Skill, but it was still a good learning experience. Though I obviously didn't hear all of it, since I was in charge of cooking and chores while they were busy training. Apparently, Amelia used Spellcraft to create a Comprehension skill that allowed her to follow along with his lectures more easily. It wasn't an all-encompassing skill like Understand Language was, but more of a learning assistant that helped her get a handle on the trickiest portions. It also seemed to help her avoid going insane from the runes, which I'd been worried about ever since Crow told us about his past pupils. He was quite a skilled teacher, even if no one could compare to Commander Saran in my eyes.

"Okay, here we are. Welcome to Uruk, the City of Water."

Amelia and I oohed and aahed along with all the other tourists around us who'd also just caught their first glimpse of the city. The place was far more spectacular than I'd imagined, with canals dotted with people in little boats running between the buildings. The canals were wide enough for the boats to seem downright tiny from a distance, and there was certainly no risk of them accidentally bumping into each other. The water in the canals was a beautiful light blue, and clear enough that you could see the bottom. I could have stood there taking in the sight of it for an entire day without getting bored. Crow, meanwhile, took one glance at our gawking faces, then turned on his heels to leave us sightseers behind.

"I'm gonna go ahead and find us an inn like we talked about, so you two feel free to take in the sights. You'll be meeting up with Lia in front of the fountain in the city's central plaza. I'll send someone there to guide you back to the inn afterward, so be there before the sun sets. Otherwise, you two can sleep in the streets for all I care," Crow said, and then promptly took his leave. Was it really wise to just leave one's friends to find their bearings in an unfamiliar city like this?

"Well, whatever. I'd say it's a good day for a date, Amelia, wouldn't you?"

"A date?"

I held out my hand, and after a bit of trepidation, she reached out and took it.

"Yeah. We can do whatever your little heart desires today. It'll be my way of rewarding you for all your hard work studying the past two weeks," I declared.

"No one's ever rewarded me for any of my achievements before," she said, her face flushing bright red as she moved to stand beside me. I smiled, trying to imagine all of the hard work she'd put in as princess of the elven people, all for the sake of her countrymen, even though she knew her work would never be properly acknowledged.

"Well, then I'm glad I could be the first... Anyway, we'd better mosey on over to where we're supposed to meet up with Lia before anything else."

As the capital city of the largest nation on the continent, Uruk was understandably vast. It would have been nice for Crow to at least point us in the right direction before heading off on his own. We didn't know left from right here, so how were we to know where the central plaza was?

"Look at that, Akira! Doesn't it look tasty?"

"Yeah, you took the words right outta my mouth."

Amelia and I had both been taken in by an enticing fragrance wafting out of a nearby shop, similar to the smell of roasted crustaceans. Though I had to imagine it probably wasn't shrimp or crab they were selling.

"Excuse me, sir—could we get two of those? And would you happen to know the way to the central fountain plaza?" I asked.

"You got it, kid! Thanks a mil! And if ya wanna get to central plaza, just head straight down that way for a good long while. Can't miss it!"

I thanked the friendly old man for the food and his help, and we chomped away at our newly acquired seafood kebabs. The meat on the skewer was called "scallop," yet it tasted like plain old grilled fish while smelling uncannily like shrimp. What a bizarre mishmash of different elements from my world. Fusion cuisine, indeed.

"Do you like it?" I asked Amelia.

"Yup. Ooh, look! Can we eat that next?"

And so our special date devolved into walking through town eating whatever interesting foods caught Amelia's fancy—not that I hadn't seen this coming when I offered to do whatever she wanted.

"Oh my gosh, Akira! Over here! This stuff looks really good too!"

Even though we were on the right path, we were taking far too many detours to make much progress. I was concerned it might be more than a little bit rude to keep a princess like Lia waiting, even if Amelia was a princess herself.

"C'mon, Akira! Over here!"

That being said, it was difficult to put an end to Amelia's fun when she was enjoying herself so much, and so we continued to make detours regardless. Though maybe this would also do a little to make up for the fact we hadn't had much quality one-on-one time ever since we left the Great Labyrinth of Kantinen, and we hadn't had much time to exchange intel recently either. I still hadn't even told her why we'd come to this city, for that matter. I was kind of planning to just go on not telling her about it too, even though we'd promised not to keep anything from each other.

"Oh! Hey, Akira, do you think *that's* the central fountain?"

Suddenly, an enormous fountain came into view—taller even than the buildings surrounding it. The fountain seemed to be the primary source for all the water flowing throughout the city, yet it also served as an iconic centerpiece for the grandeur of Uruk. About 70 percent of all the canals in the city drew from its waters. *First the Holy Tree, now this?* The scale of everything in this world was so massive compared to Japan.

"Aha! There you are! I've been waiting for you guys!" said a familiar voice, and we turned to see a peppy catgirl running our way, a friendly smile plastered across her face. "Long time no see, Princess Amelia, Akira!"

"That reminds me, Lia—that Inverted Spirit Barrier skill of yours, does it actually make use of Crow's Inversion Extra Skill? Or is that similarity just a coincidence?"

As we were riding the boat reserved explicitly for the royal family, I took the opportunity to ask a question that had been on my mind for quite some time. Because everyone knew it was a royal family boat, all the other boats made way for us to pass, and we were able to easily float down the center of the canal. The luxurious suite we were guided to within the boat was clearly designed with royal guests in mind, so I felt more than a little out of place—like a lost crow in the middle of a grand treasure chamber. Though I had to admit, the tea they served us was impeccable.

I'd been wanting to ask Lia about her barrier ever since the battle with Mahiro, but because she was already gone by the time I regained consciousness, I never got the chance to. I knew guardians like her were a class known for their defensive magic, and barriers especially. The Spirit Barrier skill she had was also well-known as the highest form of barrier magic in the world, even stronger than the high-level light magic barrier skill Sanctuary Commander Saran had used to protect us on our first trip down into a labyrinth. There was an almost divine aura of protection to it, and I had no doubt it could easily protect against any monster, even those on the deepest levels of any labyrinth.

"O-oh, no! It doesn't actually use Inversion at all—it's just a pale imitation, really!" said Lia. "I mean, sure, it was *based* on Lord Crow's skill, but the only times I've seen him use it, it happens so fast I couldn't possibly hope to emulate it myself! As you guys saw, my barrier couldn't withstand more than a single hit, so I've still got a long way to go."

It was true, her barrier *had* broken in the battle with Mahiro. But what she neglected to mention was that the one who'd broken it was also the second-strongest demon alive, so the fact it had countered even a single hit was still high praise.

"So let me get this straight: Crow's Inversion skill creates a sort of 'counter-magic' to offset and cancel out any magic spell, while your Inverted Spirit Barrier sort of does the same thing, only it can cancel out *any* attack, be it magical or physical?" I asked for clarification's sake. The way I understood it, her barrier was like a mirror. Crow was able to cancel out the enemy's spells while also casting an attack spell of his own if he so desired, while Lia was only able to reflect attacks back at the attacker. Though in certain cases, like when we were surrounded by hordes of enemies down in the Great Labyrinth of Brute, that would be of more use.

"That's correct. And I should reiterate that calling upon the power of the spirits to create barriers is no mean feat. Were I not a guardian and just a simple barrier mage, I definitely wouldn't be able to pull that off," Lia emphasized. As she told it, she had no control over how the barrier reflected the attacks. The barrier made all those decisions for her. So it really was just a facsimile of Crow's Extra Skill. "Anyway, why do you ask?" she asked with a tilt of her head.

I explained Amelia had recently learned the Inversion skill from Crow and I was just curious how the two compared, but the moment Lia heard this, she flipped.

"S-say whaaaaat?!"

The moment I saw Lia take a deep breath, I was anticipating a scream, so I'd covered my ears. Amelia, unfortunately, hadn't seen this coming and had suffered the full brunt of the auditory attack.

"Really, Akira?" Amelia said spitefully, shooting me a reproachful look. I could only smile sheepishly and shrug my shoulders.

"He *really* taught you how to use Inversion, Princess Amelia?!" asked Lia, her shoulders still trembling in disbelief.

"H-he did, yes," Amelia answered, recoiling from the sheer force of Lia's interrogation.

It felt like I was a fly on the wall watching one head of state threaten the other. Though in reality, they weren't truly on equal footing. Amelia was the rightful heir to the throne of all elfkind, while Lia was an adopted daughter of the royal family of just one beastfolk nation, without a drop of royal blood in her veins. Anyone with half a brain could tell who the more powerful princess was.

"Ahem. I beg your pardon. I shouldn't have lost my composure like that," said Lia, clearly feeling a little embarrassed. Though I could certainly understand why this revelation would be such a crushing blow, given how much respect she clearly had for Crow. "Anyway, I suppose you'll have to tell me more about that later," she continued, straightening herself. "We'll be arriving at the royal palace shortly."

"The palace? Are we being given an audience?" I asked, finding it hard to believe that any king would let a sketchy assassin like me anywhere near his castle.

"Correct. My foster father wishes to welcome Princess Amelia to our kingdom...and he'd like to speak with you as well, Akira."

Now this I was not expecting. What could the king of the largest beastfolk nation want with me? Surely he couldn't know I'd been summoned here from another world. Had he heard of my reputation as the "Silent Assassin"? I dearly hoped it was anything but that.

"I don't really know the details myself—just that he knows you're an adventurer who's earned the elven king's respect, and he has some request he'd like to make of you."

This was making less and less sense by the minute. The only way I'd earned the elven king's "respect" was by him begrudgingly allowing me to serve as Amelia's bodyguard, and that was hardly a reason to let an otherwise suspicious man with no documented background in this world into a royal palace.

"Guess I'll just have to hear it from the man himself, then," I said. We floated along in silence for a while after that, but then I remembered another question I wanted to ask Lia. "Hey, Lia, do you know a guy named Gram? Supposed to be your cousin, from what I'm told."

Lia's ears perked up, which told me she did indeed know him. Amelia, meanwhile, was stuffing her face with the teacakes lining the table as though she couldn't care less about this particular line of discussion.

"Well, I was only adopted into the royal family, and by the time I got here, Lord Gram had already left his post as prime minister, so..." she trailed off, a little wary.

"That's fine. Just tell me your general impressions of him based on your personal experience." I looked imploringly into Lia's eyes, and she finally let out a sigh and relented. Amelia and I sank deep into our chairs and prepared for a story.

"Lord Gram is the only son of King Igsam Lagoon's older sister. The current ruling family's lineage is rarely blessed with healthy births, so when Lord Gram was born, it was cause for grand celebrations."

I can already see where this is going, I thought to myself as I nabbed a cookie from the snack table.

"And since King Igsam and the rest of the royal family pampered him to no end in his youth, well...Lord Gram developed something of a superiority complex, and he quickly fell under the delusion that the entire world belonged to him."

So he got his every wish granted as a child just because he was born into a fancy palace. Must be nice to be on the winning team from birth, even if no one can decide what family they get born into.

"Eventually, he begged King Igsam to let him serve as prime minister, and after that, he was pretty much unstoppable. Women served him, children were sold by him, and men were brought in to do his dirty work. If anyone ever defied him, he'd use his personal team of mercenaries to silence them for good... The best way I can describe him is he doesn't think of anyone else as human, unless they've caught his fancy. He thinks of people like playthings."

Then his little power trip got so out of hand that they forced him to resign, and he became a guildmaster instead, eh? Lia seemed like she had more to say about Gram, but she simply stared at the ground.

"But he continued doing as he pleased, even after he was appointed as guildmaster...and now not even the king can stop him."

Now that I couldn't understand. How could the king's nephew carry more influence than the king himself?

"So they let him continue to abuse his influence as the king's nephew, even after he was essentially banished from his position of power?" asked Amelia, stealing the words right out of my mouth.

"No, the only influence Gram has the ability to use nowadays is that of any other guildmaster. It's not political strength he has anymore—it's military strength."

"Those hired mercenaries of his, you mean?" I asked.

"Correct." Lia nodded, then took a sip of tea. "I hate to say this, but...those mercenaries are far stronger than our country's strongest battalions. He uses illegal back-alley drugs to enhance their physical capabilities far beyond that of any ordinary person. I wouldn't even call them people anymore. After a few doses, they lose the ability to speak, so I highly doubt any of them lead ordinary lives. They're just mindless drones."

Lia bit her lip, and I could only imagine the things she had seen. Chances were, she'd come into direct contact with those mercenaries more than once.

"What else can you tell us about them?" asked Amelia as she crammed her mouth full with sweet after sweet. I wondered if she was even tasting them; they were probably some pretty pricey confections too, and she was just shoving them down her gullet.

"Well, from what I've seen...the way they move, it's like they don't even have control of their own bodies, which I assume is a result of the drugs. They're nothing more than killing machines designed to follow orders. While I'm by no means an expert on the subject, I am told there are indeed drugs out there capable of such a thing."

"I can't imagine they're produced by any reputable drug manufacturer," I mused, "so I'm guessing there must be someone with a chemist or pharmacist class creating and selling them on the black market. It takes a pretty unique skill set to create medicine and whatnot."

"Right. Our investigators have been looking into that too, but we haven't found any leads just yet," said Lia.

The simple existence of things like classes and stats had the ability to change our perception of the world—as I'd learned all too well since first arriving in Morrigan. After all, none of us ever would have felt we had the strength to slay monsters back in our world, and the only real difference was that now we had classes and could see our stats displayed as a number. This one little change made a world of difference; when your class was decided from birth, you didn't have to worry about what you'd be when you grew up. And since you could see your stats, you could easily see your own strengths and shortcomings. Morrigan was a far more dangerous world than ours, but it was also a lot simpler to get by in many ways. Though one thing both worlds had in common was that there was never a shortage of evil scum-bags looking for ways to use their powers for evil. And to think whoever made this drug that turned people into killing machines could have probably used those skills to save lives.

"I'm not surprised that your official investigators are having trouble digging up information, to be honest. People who get involved in shady stuff like this generally do a good job of keeping themselves hidden," I said.

"Yes, King Igsam feels the same way. If I had to guess, I'd say that's probably the main reason he's interested in enlisting your services."

As the royal palace came into view, I gazed up at it and sighed. It was time to find out if the beastfolk king's summons would be a blessing or a curse. I had no reason to suspect foul play, but I'd learned the hard way after coming to this world that you should never take a monarch at their word. I needed to stay on my guard.

The enormous building was nestled in a river valley between the mountains, and it was both far grander and far more serene than either the castle in Retice or the organic palace in the elven kingdom. I had to admit, I was expecting something a bit cruder and more boisterous from a race known primarily for short tempers.

"Welcome to the royal palace. Watch your step and be careful not to slip and fall."

Because the castle was built to straddle a river, the air was a bit humid, but not unpleasantly so. I gazed up, and had to take a moment to catch my breath—I couldn't even see the top of its tallest tower. It looked an awful lot like a certain school of witchcraft and wizardry.

"So I get that the castle's got plenty of natural protection since it's surrounded by mountains, but wouldn't you guys kinda be in trouble if enemies tried to launch an attack from the mountaintops?" I asked Lia after we stepped off the boat.

"Nope." She shook her head with a smile. "The whole place is enveloped in a huge spherical barrier from high up in the air to deep underground, so an invasion is pretty unlikely."

Judging by the smug expression on Lia's face, I assumed the barrier was one of her own spirit barriers and had been put in place by Lia herself. I looked up once again and saw the translucent membrane enclosing the castle on all sides. Was a single cast of Spirit Barrier really enough to protect an entire castle?

"Now come along, you two. King Igsam's audience chamber is right this way."

The audience chamber was an unfathomably large reception hall, much like the one we'd first been summoned into back in Retice. I had no idea what the obsession with needlessly large chambers was in this world, especially when something about the size of our student council room would have easily done the job. The only people to be found in the entire expansive chamber were the king, a lionlike beastfolk seated on his throne at the far end, and one horselike beastfolk knight standing beside him. My Detect Presence skill didn't find any hidden presences, so it really was just the five of us in the massive room. Somehow, that made me more uneasy than the alternative.

"Dear Father, I bring before you Princess Amelia Rosequartz of the Elves and her escort, the summoned hero Akira Oda, just as you requested," Lia said with a bow, and we followed suit. I had wanted to keep the fact that I was summoned from another world a secret, but it sounded like Lia had already divulged that information to her father.

The king whispered back and forth with the knight by his side for a moment before finally addressing us, at which point I lifted my head to see him grinning from ear to ear. "Oh, good, yes! Thank you, Lia. Please, come closer, all of you."

Despite his welcoming smile, there was something in his eyes that made me viscerally uncomfortable—like he was salivating at the very sight of me. I pretended I hadn't noticed anything amiss and approached the throne. The knight sized me up before letting out a pompous "hmph," making his opinion of me clear. Lia went to stand behind her father's throne as King Igsam addressed us.

"I thank you for answering my summons, Lady Amelia. And you as well, Lord Oda," he said with a merry smirk before rising from his throne. I didn't really know what the proper etiquette was when greeting a ruler of a different race, so I followed along with whatever Amelia was doing. Granted, I didn't feel the need to be especially polite since I knew he'd summoned me here to make a request of me, but I didn't want any bad behavior on my part to reflect poorly on Amelia.

"It's been quite some time, King Igsam," said Amelia.

"That it has, that it has! Say, have you given any more thought to the matter we discussed when last we saw each other?" asked the king, and Amelia's face immediately scrunched up as though she'd been forced to eat a bowl of nasty bugs. I had no idea what matter he was referring to, but it had to have been something awfully unpleasant for her to react so viscerally. But just as I was about to shrug it off as being none of my business, Amelia turned to look at me.

"I'm afraid Akira has already filled that position, Your Majesty," said Amelia, blushing up a storm.

What in the *world* were they talking about?

At this, King Igsam frowned, but quickly regained his composure. "I see. Well, that's a shame... In any case, let's dispense with the niceties and get straight to the point, shall we?" He sat back down on his throne. Not a moment later, the knight took a single step forward.

"Princess Amelia, allow me to introduce myself. My name is Victor, and I am a knight of the imperial guard, as well as His Majesty's personal knight attendant. It is a pleasure to make your acquaintance," said the horseman, bowing to Amelia with a flirtatious smile; he ignored me completely.

Amelia nodded to Victor before turning back to King Igsam. I noticed a vein popping out of Victor's head, offended at how little attention she had paid him. When the king began to speak again, I turned my attention to him.

"Firstly, I would like to thank you for aiding my daughter in the Great Labyrinth of Brute and ensuring she made it home safely. As her foster father and king of this nation, you have my deepest gratitude. Thank you," said the king as he leaned forward in reverence, but Amelia quickly shook her head.

"The incident in question only transpired because I was foolish enough to get myself kidnapped. Lia simply came into the labyrinth to rescue me. If anything, you should be thanking Crow and Akira for her safe return."

"I see. You'll have to offer Crow my thanks for his efforts, then."

Hey! Am I invisible here, or what?! I was starting to feel like I was being ignored on purpose.

"Now then. On to the other matter I wished to discuss with you today," said the king, before finally making eye contact with me. It was then that my Detect Danger skill started ringing alarm bells in my head. *Gee, thanks. Took you long enough. What a great skill—waiting to warn me until it's already too late to turn back.* "I hear you're one of the summoned heroes. Akira Oda, was it? I have a request I'd like to make of you, if you would be so kind."

"Depends on what it is," I replied, trying desperately to hold in a heavy sigh.

"How dare you speak to His Majesty so rudely!" cried Victor, incensed by my candid demeanor, and I couldn't help but let out the sigh I'd been holding in.

And here I was trying awfully hard to be polite.

"You really expect me to take on a request without even hearing what it is? Tell me the details of the job and what you're offering me first, then we'll talk," I said, and King Igsam gave a weak little smile.

"It seems our hero from another world is shrewder than we anticipated. Very well, then... I would like you to perform an assassination for me. As recompense, I can offer you guaranteed safety for as long as you are within our borders."

When I saw the smirk plastered across the king's face, it struck me that this man was the exact kind of person I hated most.

"Sorry, no deal."

"Wha?!" Victor gasped as his eyes shot wide open. I wasn't sure if the beastfolk people saw their king as a god or something, but he sure seemed surprised that anyone would dare to say no to him.

"And why not?" asked the king. "I've heard you've been attacked by countless monsters and villains ever since arriving in this world. Not just by those bandits in the elven domain, but in Ur and Mali as well. I was under the impression that one's personal security and freedom were what mattered most to you people who come from a world of safety and comfort, where war and strife are all but nonexistent."

I wasn't sure where this guy had gotten his information about our world, but he had some serious misconceptions.

"No offense, but I can take care of myself, thanks. I don't need your protection."

Maybe he didn't realize how high-level I was, but just from checking the stats pages of various people around the palace, I knew no one here could hold a candle to me. To be fair, they had no way of seeing my stats. However, if he was so familiar with the attacks we'd faced, shouldn't he also have heard how I'd wiped entire hordes of monsters off the map with ease?

"Yeah, right, kid!" Victor scoffed. "I bet you started the rumors about how easily you wiped out the monsters in Ur yourself!"

I could certainly understand the unruly horseman's doubts. The average citizen who knew nothing about my Shadow Magic and hadn't been there to witness it themselves would have a hard time believing so many monsters could have been swallowed up in the blink of an eye.

"Wow, so you're calling him a liar?" Amelia chimed in with a frown. "And what exactly gives you reason to believe the rumors aren't true, hm?"

"Well, what makes *you* so sure he's not making it up?! They say you were kidnapped at the time, so you couldn't have been around to see it! There's no way a shrimp like him could have killed more than a hundred monsters with a wave of his hand!"

It seemed we had devolved into judging people by appearances. Where did this guy get off? King Igsam, meanwhile, was doing nothing to reel his man in, just watching the proceedings with an interested grin. Out of the corner of my eye, I saw Amelia's scowl deepen. I wasn't sure I'd ever seen her so pissed off before.

"The fact that you even got word of the attack implies there were people there who saw it firsthand and lived to tell about it. Do you not believe a word your fellow knights tell you either? And as it happens, I think I know Akira's abilities far better than someone who only met him today. So do us all a favor and keep that mouth of yours shut. Your pathetic bickering is starting to get on my nerves."

Hot damn. I felt like I had just witnessed a murder. Never before had I seen a man get so thoroughly destroyed with words.

Her skill with words was evidence of her having lived longer than anyone else in the room. Victor gritted his teeth in silent anguish.

"I cannot speak to the validity of any rumors about Akira's actions that day, as I was not there to witness them myself," Amelia continued. "However, it should go without saying that my absence does not make Akira a liar. As such, this line of discussion is pointless and unproductive...so let's return to the matter at hand, shall we? Who exactly is it that you want Akira to assassinate?"

Right, I'd totally forgotten about the assassination gig. I guess I got a little too distracted by him insinuating I couldn't protect myself.

"As you are both adventurers yourselves, I'm sure you'll already be familiar with his name," the king began, "but the man I'd like you to assassinate is the guildmaster of the Uruk branch—Gram."

And there it is. I heard Lia gasp in surprise. Amelia and I reacted similarly.

"So you want to put out a hit on your own nephew," I stated.

This was quite the request. Hired by a king to kill a member of the royal family. I wasn't a citizen of his country, so he couldn't order me to do it, yet I still felt a certain compulsion to give it some serious consideration due to his legal power. It put me in an awkward position.

"So you already know of Gram. Good, that will expedite things. Kill him, and in exchange, I will guarantee your safety."

"Were you even listening to me?" I asked. "I'm strong enough to defend myself, and I don't do hit jobs."

He was starting to get on my nerves now, but just as I was about to lose my temper, Amelia grabbed me by the hand.

"Then how about this?" she suggested. "Why don't you have the strongest soldier in the entire castle come down here and fight Akira. If Akira happens to lose, then we will accept your terms. But if he wins, you will let us leave here in peace. Would that be all right with you, Akira?"

I nodded, then looked up at the throne.

"Are you sure about this, Lady Amelia? He may be a summoned hero, but there's no way he could win against a beastman," said the king, his elbows propped on the throne's armrests.

Finally, it was all starting to make sense. In this world, demons were the top dogs, followed by elves and beastfolk, with humans as the weakest race of all. This universal understanding was both why Victor doubted me over trusting his informant's words, and why King Igsam offered safety instead of any monetary reward. It was all because I was a human, and humans were weak.

"That's where you're wrong," I told him. "I'm also not the kind of guy who backs down when someone calls me a liar in front of the woman I love."

"Then I do hope you won't regret making a fool of yourself in front of her when you lose."

Not wanting to do battle in such a fine building, we all went out to the castle courtyard. As we stepped up onto a raised platform, I got my first good look at Victor, and I was a little taken aback. Earlier, the lower half of his body had been hidden from view behind the throne, yet now I could see it all.

"A centaur, eh...?"

He was not just a horseman—he was half man, half horse. I'd seen an awful lot of beastfolk since arriving in Brute, but never one that seemed so much more "beast" than "man." Most just looked like humans with a few little beastlike traits and facial features, but this guy was full-on horse from the waist down.

I wasn't sure how word had spread so quickly, but a rather large crowd had gathered to watch the duel—there were so many spectators that I had to wonder if they'd been waiting in the wings for something like this to happen. The palace was a place of quiet serenity, yet this one small part was in an absolute uproar. The vast majority of the audience seemed to be soldiers, though there were a fair few government officials in attendance too, and I wondered if they should really be watching this while on the clock. I didn't know what this world's obsession with duels was, but apparently they were a major form of entertainment. I could kind of understand the fascination in Brute, given the stereotypes about beastfolk temperaments, but it seemed bizarre that even the peace-loving elves had jumped at the chance to hold a duel while I was there.

When King Igsam (with Lia and Amelia in tow) walked out onto the second-floor balcony, a hush immediately fell over the rambunctious audience. They were far more disciplined and orderly than the king's soldiers back in the castle of Retice, that much was for sure. Usually men like them couldn't help but make a stir upon seeing Amelia's face for the first time.

"Now then. We are gathered here today to bear witness to an auspicious bout between the summoned hero, Akira Oda, and the castle's finest soldier, our very own Victor."

Hearing that Victor was supposedly the strongest fighter in the castle came as a bit of a surprise. He had initially struck me as the type of workhorse who would spend all day hunched over a desk writing reports, and I could see many soldiers in the crowd far more muscular than him. *Can't judge a book by its cover, I suppose.*

The crowd whispered among themselves upon hearing I was a summoned hero, which didn't surprise me. After all, aside from myself and the hero's party, all of my other classmates were still locked up tight in Retice, and no one really knew whether they were alive or dead. There were even rumors circulating that the recent hero summoning ritual had been a complete failure, and that Retice was just trying to hide it.

"On my name as Igsam Lagoon, King of the great beastfolk nation of Uruk, I do hereby recognize this bout not as a simple squabble between individuals, but as an officially sanctioned duel. Duelists, take your positions and prepare for battle."

As Victor rested his massive battle-ax on his shoulders, I drew the two daggers made from the remains of the Yato-no-Kami and held them in a backhanded grip.

"Let the duel begin!" King Igsam declared from his perch on the balcony.

Immediately, Victor rushed across the platform, hooves pounding as he closed the distance and swung his mighty battle-ax downward.

"Whuh-oh. That was a close one," I said. *Psych*. I could've dodged his attack in my sleep, but the crowd sounded impressed.

"Whoa! How the hell did he dodge that?!"

"I'm not even sure *I* could have dodged that one..."

After whiffing his first attack, Victor put distance between us again and we both circled the edges of the arena, staring each other down.

"When I first heard them talking about the assassin who fights like a warrior, I thought it was the dumbest thing I'd ever heard, but it seems you really do know a thing or two," Victor muttered under his breath. I was a little surprised that he would try to strike up a conversation, but I remained on my guard, awaiting his next move. "However...let's see you try to dodge *this*!"

He swung his battle-ax with even greater speed than last time, but once again, I side-stepped it quite easily. Only this time, Victor predicted followed through on his swing.

"Hup!"

Not in the mood to be cleaved in half, I jumped out of the way of the oncoming attack and landed right on top of the blade of Victor's ax.

"Wha?!" he blustered.

"Hiyah!"

I dove and swung my dagger at Victor's throat, but he quickly pulled his battle-ax back in to deflect it. After a smooth midair recovery, I landed on the ground a safe distance away, but before I had a chance to catch my breath, Victor charged, his ax raised high overhead.

"Whoa! That little guy jumps around like a freaking acrobat!"

"He's so fast, it's insane!"

"Dang, I didn't even see it..."

As the crowd oohed and aahed, the battle-ax came down and clashed with both my daggers. I may not have been able to match the burly physique of my opponent, but I still managed to come out of the blade lock on top. With as much force as I could muster, I pushed my daggers up, and Victor's ax went flying high into the air before coming back down and burying its blade in the ground.

"Th-that's enough!" King Igsam cried as I thrust my daggers at Victor, who had fallen backward onto the ground.

I looked up to the second-floor balcony and made eye contact with Amelia. She was mouthing words to me—"don't be such a show-off," maybe? Apparently, she'd realized I was biding my time, but I hadn't felt like it would be right to end the duel in the first second without giving the audience a little bit of a show. Naturally, Amelia had seen right through my charade.

"Hey, can you stand?" I asked, reaching a hand down to help Victor up off the ground. He'd been muttering incredulously, clearly not believing a human had defeated a powerful centaur like him.

"Don't touch me!" he snarled, slapping my hand away.

"Keep your filthy human mitts off me! How could a miserable runt like you beat *me*?! How?!"

His eyes were bloodshot, and his previous cool composure was nowhere to be seen. I was confused. Had I really offended

him so badly? A few of his fellow soldiers dragged him kicking and screaming back into the castle, while the remaining soldiers gathered around me, and one apologized on Victor's behalf.

"Sorry about that. Victor's a really good guy, but he had a pretty negative encounter with some humans a long time ago, and he always gets like this whenever one of your kind tries to touch him. He's usually fine as long as you keep your distance, so feel free to talk to him later."

"All right. Will do." I nodded. Apparently, he was well-loved by his fellow knights. And if there'd been a traumatic incident in his past, I couldn't hold it against him. Something told me he did bear at least a *little* bit of a personal grudge against me, but I decided to leave it alone.

"But man, those moves of yours were insane!"

"Yeah, that was crazy! You should spar with me next!"

"No, me first!"

"S-sure, no problem. Go ahead and come at me; I can take you all on at once, if you like," I said, and the soldiers let out a cheer. *Sheesh.*

I knew that beastfolk loved a good fight, but I never would have expected them to actually *relish* the opportunity to get their asses handed to them. I hoped fighting them wouldn't constitute a violation of duel sanctity or anything like that, but since there were some high-ranking officials watching, it was probably fine. Four of the soldiers stepped up onto the platform to face me as the others watching down below began to titter with excitement.

"Good day to you all! My name is Tomaz, and as the commander of Uruk's 55th Knights Squadron, I shall serve as referee! If any of you manage to incapacitate Lord Oda, I'll treat you to one of my prized bottles of liquor! Show him what you're made of, everyone!"

"Ohhh! Commander Tomaz must be in a good mood today!"

"Hey, can I fight in the next match?! Can I?!"

Before I knew it, an incentive had been slapped on my friendly sparring match; predictably, this made more people want to try their luck against me. I didn't have all day to play around. If we didn't make it back to the central fountain before sunset, we'd be sleeping on the streets. I looked up to the second-floor balcony in hopes that Amelia, Lia, or even the king might bail me out, but they were nowhere to be seen. I could have also used some emotional support.

"Let the battles begin!"

Right when the referee gave the signal, I activated Conceal Presence. I didn't have time to waste, so I wanted to get this over with as quickly as possible.

"Whoa, did he just disappear?!"

"Must be some sort of skill!"

"Hey! Does anyone have Illusion Breaker?!"

As the soldiers swung their weapons wildly through the empty air, I snuck up behind the man with the highest stats in the current group. After a firm karate chop to the back of his neck, he sputtered out a groan and fell to the ground, unconscious.

"Look out, folks! Commander Gen is already down for the count! Didn't even have a chance to say uncle! Only three fighters remain! Who will be the one to take out the assassin?! Hey, can someone drag Commander Gen off the stage?!"

Wow, this is turning into quite the event. We've even got an announcer now. I dashed over and rammed the hilt of my dagger into the gut of the second-strongest fighter, who keeled over with a guttural moan.

"And there goes Captain Adolph! Only two challengers left now!"

Okay, I guess I should probably turn off Conceal Presence now. Wouldn't be very fair to finish this whole thing without showing myself when the crowd's getting so hyped up.

"Look out, folks! Lord Oda has deactivated his skill and made himself visible again! Now's your chance—go get him!" cried the increasingly biased announcer; having a biased referee wouldn't make a difference.

"Nothing personal, little guy..."

"...but this ends here!"

The two remaining challengers came at me in tandem, almost as though they'd rehearsed the move. I couldn't blame them for teaming up at this point.

"Nice try, guys." I cleanly dodged both of their attacks and delivered a swift chop to each of their necks. Just like a sword-fight straight out of the movies, they remained standing for a few seconds after the dust settled before collapsing to their knees. I didn't know such a thing was even possible in real life. I'd always thought it looked kinda corny.

"That's it, folks! Lord Oda remains undefeated!"

Per Amelia's advice, I'd begun making a habit of checking everyone's stats, and doing so had definitely helped me decide who to take out first in the fight. However, using it for extended periods of time or on moving targets gave me a massive headache. I had to take care not to leave it on for too long, but I'd definitely come to appreciate it more as an invaluable asset in battle.

As the unconscious combatants were dragged off the stage, five more hopeful challengers stepped up to take their place. I let out a sigh. It seemed there was no end to the amount of soldiers who wished to try their luck against me. And here I was hoping I'd have a chance to ask King Igsam a few questions, but it was starting to look like we might not make it back in time for the sunset rendezvous that Crow had arranged for us.

"You think we'll make it in time, Akira?"

"Hard to say, really."

I'd spent the rest of the afternoon knocking out each and every challenger without breaking a sweat. Afterward, I had to turn down an invitation to go drinking with some high-ranking soldiers. No matter how many times I told them I was underage, they didn't get the message (apparently, there was no such thing as a drinking age here), so I eventually just made up something about how humans weren't really supposed to drink alcohol and slipped away when Lia showed up and distracted them. If it hadn't been for them, we would have made it out of the palace a hell of a lot earlier. The sun had already begun to set, and our boat was moving awfully slow. Even going as fast as we could in a royal vessel (which they'd been kind enough to lend us) straight down the middle of the canal, I wasn't sure we'd make it in time.

"I guess I didn't really get much of a chance to make good on my date offer today, did I?" I said as I fell down on the comfortable couch, realizing I'd promised Amelia we could do whatever she wanted today.

Amelia simply smiled and shook her head. "It's been a long time since I got to see you fight like that."

Had it been that long? I cocked my head and tried to remember. Before we came to Uruk, there'd been the beauty pageant in Mali, and before that, the last time I'd drawn my weapon around her was when it had been refashioned into a pair of daggers.

"I like watching you fight, Akira. You looked so cool out there today."

I was not expecting a compliment, and I covered my mouth and turned away to hide my surprise. I didn't want Amelia to see the look on my face. Not that I had a mirror handy, but I probably looked pretty lame.

"Yeah? Glad to hear it," I managed to say, trying to play it cool as Amelia sat down beside me. Even without looking at her, I knew the bewitching smile she had to be wearing.

"I'm glad I came on this journey with you, Akira. If I had stayed home in the elven domain, there's no way I would've enjoyed this much excitement. Not to mention all the delicious food, of course, but more than anything, I just love being around you. When I'm with you, Akira, every day is a treat...so thanks. For dragging me along with you."

Great, things were getting even more embarrassing. But I felt like I owed her a genuine response, so I swallowed my embarrassment and turned to face her.

"I didn't drag you into anything. You were the one who said you wanted to come with me. You chose a path for yourself and then followed it. If anything, I'm the one who should be thanking you for choosing to spend time with a schmuck like me instead of your family. Thanks, Amelia."

"Wow, Akira. How do you always know exactly what to say to soothe my anxiety?"

"Couldn't tell you... Now, c'mon, we're almost to the central fountain. We'd better get ready to disembark."

Amelia nodded and I took her by the hand. We headed out onto the deck to see a beautiful red sunset just like the ones I'd known in Japan. It seemed like we might just make our rendezvous yet.

POV: AMELIA ROSEQUARTZ

THE MOMENT Akira won the duel, King Igsam was in visible distress.

"Impossible... How could a human defeat a beastman? It defies all logic!"

Lia, having witnessed Akira's strength firsthand down in the Great Labyrinth of Brute, didn't seem fazed in the slightest, but this only served to make King Igsam's overreaction stand out all the more.

"Why are you so agitated about this, Your Majesty? This was to be expected, especially considering Akira defeated my older sister. And since you seem to be well-informed about our journey, it's rather odd that you wouldn't know about the Kilika incident," I said, and King Igsam remained silent, all but confirming my suspicions. "In fact, it seems the only intel you have on us is about encounters we had with your fellow beastfolk. Do you mind explaining why that is?"

I'd overheard Akira talking about the traffickers we'd encountered in the elven domain bearing the crest of Uruk on their swords, and that while Gram was apparently the one who'd hired them, they could have very well been soldiers of this very kingdom. I didn't want to believe King Igsam was capable of directing his men to kidnap my elven countrymen, but if there was even the slightest chance he could put Akira in danger, I had to explore every avenue. I wasn't about to let anyone lay a finger on Akira—not a king, not even a god.

King Igsam stepped away from the balcony and took a seat on a luxurious couch in the next room. "Very well. Have a seat right there. Lia, would you be a dear and ask them to bring up a few drinks for us?" asked the king.

"As you wish, Father," Lia replied and dutifully left the room.

I sat down in the chair opposite King Igsam as he began to speak. "First off, why don't you tell me everything you already know about Gram?"

"I know he's your sister's son, and that he was very pampered in his youth, as historically it's been difficult for the royal family to have children. And that he took advantage of this special treatment and used his authority to do whatever he pleased with the kingdom. And that this continues to this day, even though he's been demoted to a simple guildmaster. He has his fingers in the illegal drug trade, and not even you can stop him, Your Majesty," I said, summarizing the information Lia had given us on the boat ride to the palace.

King Igsam grimaced, but nodded. "That's correct. Even with the royal army under my direct command, I cannot hope to win against Gram's drug-enhanced mercenaries. And while the bandits who attacked you in the elven kingdom were originally my soldiers, I lost them to Gram's drugs as well. I like to think I'm starting to get a handle on telling which soldiers are being controlled from those who aren't, but honestly, it's extremely difficult to tell. I am at a loss. That boy has always been clever, ever since he was a child, and he's thoroughly outmaneuvered me."

"Then why did you want to hire Akira to assassinate Gram? Considering you clearly had no faith in his abilities."

Surely a king would have at least a few assassins at his beck and call; no country the size of Uruk was built without some hands getting dirty.

"Because if a member of my assassin corps were to fail and word got out that they were under my employ, it could very well be grounds for a coup. That assassin friend of yours doesn't have a paper trail they could follow, as he's not even from this world. If he were to fail and get himself killed, it's highly unlikely anyone could trace him back to me. What better option do I have?"

I didn't like his answer, but I did recognize kings were often forced to make difficult decisions—but whether something was understandable and whether it was ethical were two entirely different things.

"Akira would never let you use him as a means to illicit ends. But assume he did submit to your demands, and then later made it back to his world and told them of his experiences here. Would you really want to make an enemy of a man from a world that, by all accounts, is far more technologically advanced than our own? What if they developed a way to come and go from our world as they pleased? Should they ever desire to launch an offensive against us, our world would surely fall into ruin."

"Pfft... Heh heh... Ah ha ha ha!" the king chortled. "It is easy to tell how advanced his world must be just from looking at the way he performs, but the scenario you describe is simply not possible. Such a future will never come to pass."

I tilted my head, confused. I'd heard King Igsam's birth class was a simple scribe—certainly not the sort of person who could tell the future with any definitive accuracy. But as I sat there wondering what made him so sure, he laughed in my face.

"Some things are simply beyond the realm of possibility, my dear. He and his fellow heroes are destined to live out the rest of their days in this world, never returning to their own... It's admirable to have a dream you feel is worth pursuing—how tragically beautiful it is to work your entire life for something that will remain forever out of reach."

I'd only met King Igsam previously at diplomatic events I'd attended with my father, so he certainly wasn't a man I was intimately familiar with, but I was starting to get a feel for what sort of person he truly was. I could also see how a villain like Gram could have come from the same family. They were both wretched people, plain and simple.

"In any event," the king went on, "I think it's high time you started thinking seriously about your future, Princess. While I'm not saying it's your fault this boy decided to whisk you away from the elven domain, you need to remember you are the next in line to the elven throne, not some errant hero's plaything."

His words felt like a slap across the face. Of course I knew many people had expectations of me as next in line to the throne, even if I had no interest in succeeding my father, but to imply I was nothing more than a plaything to Akira was out of line. Nor had he "whisked me away"—I had come along of my own volition. I wanted to scream it in this man's face, but the words would not come. It seemed no matter where we went, people only believed I was with Akira because he'd coerced me, and I had to wonder if this would bring Akira more problems in the long run.

"I apologize for the delay, Father," said Lia, reentering the room. "We were all out of tea, so I brought some lemon water instead."

"Oh, you don't say? We'll need to send someone out to buy more, then."

"Indeed. Princess Amelia, it's getting late. Allow me to see you to the docks," said Lia, her complexion pale. I nodded and rose from my chair.

"If you'll excuse me, Your Highness."

"Yes, yes. Goodbye now."

In the end, I didn't get to say a single word in my defense.

"Um... Princess Amelia?" Lia asked as we were walking down the corridor, trepidation written all over her face. She stopped walking, so I did as well.

"What is it?"

"W-well, I hope you'll forgive me, but I actually eavesdropped on your entire conversation," Lia admitted, hanging her head low.

I started walking again, and Lia scrambled to catch up with me. I didn't have Akira's Detect Presence skill, so I couldn't be sure how long she'd been eavesdropping, but when she entered the room at such a perfect moment in my conversation with the king, I knew she'd overheard at least some of what was said.

"It's fine... Tell me, Lia: What do you think? Does it seem like I'm being dragged around by Akira against my will?"

Lia mulled this over before giving a slight nod with a miffed expression. "I know this might just be my own internalized prejudice talking, but when I see a summoned hero walking around with an elven woman so far from the Sacred Forest, even though all my life I've been told no elf would willingly leave their homeland...there are only two possibilities that come to mind. Either he's enlisted her as a party member under the pretense of defeating the Demon Lord, leaving her no choice but to accept...or he kidnapped her to keep him company. But my father knows of your combat prowess, Princess Amelia, so I'm sure he assumed it was the former."

In other words, he thought I only agreed to be Akira's party member to save face, and he was taking pity on me.

"B-but it's not like everyone assumes that! I know you're not being held against your will, and so do all the other women here in the palace!" Lia added in a fluster, before glancing down at my left hand. "I mean, that 'ring' on your fourth finger is supposed to be symbolic of eternal love and happiness, right?! Akira has the same scar on his left hand, and I know a lot of couples here in the castle have done the same ritual, so it's plain to see your love is genuine!" There was a twinkle in Lia's eyes as she spoke.

I hadn't realized it was so widespread, to be honest. When Akira and I exchanged rings, we'd been caught up in the heat of the moment and hadn't really considered how the scar might sting the morning after, or in the bath. Had we considered those things at the time, we might have hesitated a bit before making the cuts. "You mean it's a relatively common practice?" I asked, surprised.

"Yep! I heard it all started because people saw something similar in a book that made its way over here from Kantinen. It was all the rage with humans when it came out, and now it's making waves with readers over here in Brute too!"

Just as I was about to ask if Lia had read it, we arrived at the courtyard where Akira was presumed to be.

"Aw, c'mon! One or two little drinks won't hurt ya!"

"Yeah, a little drinking never hurt nobody! All the cool kids are doing it!"

"I told you, I don't drink!"

In the middle of all the ruckus in the courtyard, I found Akira being accosted by the country's military officials.

"Yeah, so a bunch of soldiers asked to spar with Akira after the duel, and now it sounds like they all wanna go out and get wasted with him," Lia explained, and I was reminded there was a legal drinking age back in Akira's world. "But hey, at least they've taken a shine to him, I guess!"

"Besides, I need to get back before sunset or else I'll be sleeping on the streets tonight. Now would you guys *please* get out of my way?!" Akira said as he tried to push his way through the crowd of soldiers, but there were simply too many of them for him to make much headway.

"Okay, I'll try to keep the soldiers occupied, so you and Akira make a break for the docks, okay? I'll come and visit you guys at the inn tomorrow!" shouted Lia before running into the crowd of soldiers. She didn't even wait for my response. "General Zarrus! Did you already finish your duties for the day?"

"L-Lady Lia..."

The generals quieted upon noticing Lia's presence.

"And you, General Cylla! Didn't your wife order you to lay off the booze?" Lia asked.

"Damn it, Liura... You ratted me out to the princess?!"

As Lia kept the generals' attention, Akira finally managed to slip out from the crowd of soldiers.

"Uh-oh, fellas! Looks like the top brass is in for another one of Lady Lia's infamous lectures!"

"God, she's so cute when she's putting the generals in their place..."

I knew Lia was supposed to be "just" an adopted member of the royal family, but it seemed the people living in the castle had taken a genuine liking to her. I found it rather amusing how they treated her less like a cute little sister and more like a strict maternal figure.

"Akira, we need to leave right now if you want to sleep in a bed tonight," I told him.

Akira nodded and grabbed me by the hand, then we dashed out of the courtyard. As we ran, I looked down at our clasped hands and the ring mark on Akira's finger. The cut had been quite deep, so it was still an angry red and plain to see. As was the matching scar on my ring finger.

"Keep up, Amelia—we've gotta go!"

I gave Akira's hand a little squeeze and held on tight.

All we had to do was say Lia's name down at the docks, and they guided us to a boat that had already been prepared for us to borrow. Akira immediately crashed on one of the onboard couches and let out a heavy sigh.

"I guess I didn't really get much of a chance to make good on my date offer today, did I?" he lamented as he caught his breath.

I shook my head. "It's been a long time since I got to see you fight like that. I like watching you fight, Akira. You looked so cool out there today," I said with a smile, and Akira turned away sheepishly.

"Yeah? Glad to hear it," he said.

He was so cute when he was embarrassed. Feeling like teasing him a little more, I sat down on the couch beside him, leaned forward, and tried to get a good look at his face. I couldn't see much, but through the gaps in his hair I could see even his ears were flushed bright red.

"I'm glad I came on this journey with you, Akira. If I had stayed home in the elven domain, there's no way I would've enjoyed this much excitement. Not to mention all the delicious food, of course, but more than anything, I just love being around you. When I'm with you, Akira, every day is a treat...so thanks. For dragging me along with you."

When the king had implied I was just Akira's plaything, it genuinely took me by surprise. But when I really thought about it, I probably never would have left the Sacred Forest had it not been for Akira, and I wanted to express my thanks.

"I didn't drag you into anything. You were the one who said you wanted to come with me. You chose a path for yourself and then followed it. If anything, I'm the one who should be thanking you for choosing to spend time with a schmuck like me instead of your family. Thanks, Amelia."

King Igsam's words must have been gnawing at my brain more than I realized, because this reassurance from Akira made me immeasurably happy. I could even feel myself blushing. "Wow, Akira. How do you always know exactly what to say to soothe my anxiety?"

"Couldn't tell you... Now c'mon, we're almost to the central fountain. We'd better get ready to disembark."

Akira, still a little red in the face, took me by the hand and led me out to the deck just in time to see the sun begin to set behind the city's central fountain. It looked like we were going to make it there in time after all, and for that, I was enormously grateful.

My Status as an Assassin Obviously Exceeds the Hero's

CHAPTER 4

New Revelations

POV: ODA AKIRA

"LADY AMELIA and Lord Akira, I presume?"

At the central fountain, in almost the same spot we'd found Lia that morning, we were greeted by a man in a butler uniform. Startled, Amelia and I looked at each other.

"Yeah, that's us," I said.

The man sighed in relief and bowed his head. "I am on orders from Lord Crow to lead you both back to the inn. My name is Emile."

He bowed his head again, and the tension left my shoulders; there was always some anxiety whenever someone you didn't know addressed you by name.

"It's a little bit of a walk from here. The ground is also quite slippery, so do watch your step," Emile said.

Even this city of water had sidewalks for pedestrians, as well as bridges dotted here and there crossing the canals. This led to a confusing network of intersecting pathways, and since all of the buildings adhered to the same general architecture and coloring, it was unreasonable to expect any first-time visitor to find their way around the city on foot without a guide. Apparently, a retired adventurer tried to make a map of this labyrinthine city once, but he got so discouraged by its complexity that he gave up after a year and change. However, thanks to his efforts, a basic outline of the major roads and landmarks was made, which led to a huge boom in tourism, so his work was not for nothing. Emile told us all of this as we made our way to the inn, before revealing he was the grandson of said adventurer.

"My grandfather always used to say, 'There is nothing you can't achieve through hard work and determination, except when it comes to that blasted city.' I hope the two of you will be careful not to lose your way if you ever decide to go out on the town alone."

After about a twenty-minute walk, we arrived at the entrance to our lodgings in the middle of a ritzy hotel district. The building was so tall that even attempting to see the top made my neck hurt.

"Welcome to the Caesar Hotel. We're so very honored to have not only the elven princess, but a summoned hero gracing our humble establishment."

When I saw they had lined up the entire staff just to greet us as though this were a traditional Japanese inn, I wanted to do an about-face and walk right out the door. First the Hotel Raven, and now this—why did Crow only choose hotels fancy enough to make a scrub like me feel extremely out of place?

"Aren't you coming, Akira?"

"Er, yeah, sorry. Be right there."

At the very least, we could be sure to sleep soundly in any hotel selected by Crow. The man had connections. We were led up to a glamorous room on the top floor that was clearly intended for more than three people. I didn't even want to know what the nightly rate was.

"Oh, good. There you guys are," said Crow, greeting us between sips of tea.

"What is it with you and picking only the fanciest-schmanciest hotels, man? We're not *made* of money, you know," I said as I set down the luggage I'd been carrying, and Amelia nodded in agreement. That was somewhat amusing, since Amelia's expensive appetite was a big reason for our dwindling funds.

"Don't worry about that. This place owes me a favor."

So he was just walking around the city looking for a place that would let us stay for free, then? How many hotel owners were in this one man's debt?

"I've stopped an awful lot of hotel bar fights in my day. During this one, though, I'm pretty sure a rival company, jealous of how well these guys were doing, released a bucking bronco into the lobby to try to trash the place, and I stopped it."

Damn. That went beyond simple harassment—that was actual property damage. I wondered what the punishment was for something like that in this world. In Japan, that'd be grounds to press charges, but over here, the law wasn't so rigid. Morrigan was a world where there was no standard procedure for judgment and prosecution, not even for murderers. I wondered what it felt like to only have a vague idea of what constituted a crime. I'd been in this world for quite some time now, and to me it felt like there really weren't any universal sets of rules, spoken or otherwise.

"How did you ever stop that?" I asked, genuinely curious.

"I got the horse pinned down, and luckily someone nearby was a vet and had some horse tranquilizers handy, so he helped knock the sucker out."

It would take an awful lot of strength to pin down a bucking bronco. Granted, my impression of Crow's physical abilities was pretty high, but I couldn't even imagine how strong he must have been in his heyday. It was sure convenient that there had been a vet with horse tranquilizers right nearby.

"What happened to the rival company?" I asked.

"They're still kicking around, right across the street. Their reputation took a massive hit, though."

As Crow and I chatted about ultimately pointless things, I noticed Amelia starting to nod off, then realized it was well past her normal bedtime.

"If you're sleepy, Amelia, you can go on ahead into the bedroom and get some rest," I told her.

"R-right..." she murmured, rubbing her eyes but making no attempt to move.

"C'mon, quit rubbing your eyes. You'll only make 'em red."

"Mmnh... Akira, carry me..."

Amelia turned quite needy when she got sleepy, and I was fortunate to have grown up with a clingy younger sister—it allowed me to put Amelia to sleep when she got like this without feeling any undue urges. As I cradled Amelia in my arms, Crow and I resumed our conversation. Her body heat helped ward off the chill of the hotel room.

"You're a lot like an elf, you know that?" said Crow, possibly referring to my hunger for knowledge in all its forms.

He may have a point. I chuckled softly to myself, readjusting my hold on Amelia.

"When I look at you, I'm reminded of a man I once knew. He wasn't an elf either, but he loved to ask all sorts of questions, just like you," Crow went on, a sad look on his face. "You're both like sponges who wanna suck up as much knowledge as they can, desperate for anything new, almost like you think you're gonna die tomorrow."

I couldn't help but glare at Crow.

"I know, I know. You don't intend to come off that way, but that's how this other guy always seemed to me—he was so dedicated to his pursuit of knowledge that people started calling him a 'sage' eventually. He was the sort of guy who could look at the exact same thing you're looking at and see it on two or three deeper levels than you ever could. Shame I never got to say goodbye to him, though I never got to say goodbye to my own sister either, so maybe I'm just unlucky like that."

Was Crow implying he hadn't been able to say goodbye to a friend on his deathbed? It was a little strange to hear Crow calling *anyone* a friend. Maybe I was biased, but he struck me as the sort of guy who preferred to be alone, but apparently, I was wrong. As I leaned forward to pour myself some tea, I decided to casually inquire as to who this other person (who apparently resembled me so much) actually was.

"What was his name?" I asked as I shifted Amelia to my lap and poured myself some tea.

Crow took a moment to think about it. Could he really not recall this supposed "old friend's" name without mulling it over? "Let's see, uh... Saran Mithray, I believe it was. Been so long since I saw the guy that I almost completely forgot, heh."

My teacup fell from my hand, and the contents spilled all over the table. It didn't make a very loud noise, but it still managed to wake Amelia. I was so stunned, I barely noticed.

"What did you just say?" I asked.

"I said the man's name was Saran Mithray. He had golden hair, an almost frustratingly handsome face, and while he always acted like an ignorant old geezer, he was actually quite the cunning mage, specializing in light magic... Why do you ask? Did you know him?"

I'd thought maybe I'd misheard him, but with the added description, it was clear Crow was talking about the same Saran I'd known and not someone else with the same name.

"But wait a minute, how could you know Saran? Where did you two meet?" Crow asked before I even had the chance to answer his first question. He seemed to have assumed that I really did know the man, perhaps due to our similar personalities, but he was now dubious as to how that would even be possible. To be fair, it did seem a little outlandish for someone so new to this world to just randomly have met one of Crow's old friends. It was quite the coincidence.

Amelia chimed in then, saying, "All I know about the 'sage' known as Saran Mithray is that even the Demon Lord acknowledged his abilities, and that he was a famous wanderer who never stayed in one place for very long. When I heard Akira say that a man by that name had been his mentor, I found it very strange. He didn't sound like the type of person to take on pupils to me. So I thought maybe it was someone with the same name, but Akira never wanted to talk about him much, so I didn't pry. Hard to believe you knew him too, Crow..."

"Well, the man Crow described sounds like the Commander Saran I knew, and it's not like there are many light mages out there to begin with. We must be talking about the same guy," I concluded. Though I found it a bit hard to believe Saran was so famous, especially if he didn't stay in one place for long.

"Okay, let's back up a bit and review what we know," said Crow, trying to get us all to calm down a bit. He handed me a fresh cup of tea, which I sipped to calm myself. I wasn't the biggest fan of black tea, but it did seem to help me relax, as my flustered brain quickly fell back into listening mode. "For starters, the Saran I knew never stayed in one place for long, *but* he also went completely off the grid a while ago. And you called him 'Commander' Saran, correct?"

"Yeah." I nodded. "He was the Kingdom of Retice's Knight Commander."

"Oh, then he must've been Gilles's superior too. The subject never really came up, but I guess there wasn't much of a reason for it to, especially since we fell out of touch for a good while. Hard to believe Saran became a knight of all things... Doesn't sound like him at all," Crow said. He rested his elbows on the table and gazed at me inquisitively. "How much did you know about him?"

"I'm not sure what you're asking," I replied, taking another sip of my tea and grimacing at the bitterness.

"Maybe you aren't aware of this, but every time someone says the name 'Saran,' you immediately tense up and give off some serious murderous vibes. Do you know something about how he died that I should be aware of?"

Observant as ever, this one. Or perhaps I was just much too easy to read. "I mean, yeah, you could definitely say that... It was my fault that he died, after all."

We'd been traveling with Crow for a decent while now, but this was the first time I'd ever spoken with him about my first weeks after being summoned to this world. Hell, I'd only even talked about it to *Amelia* once before, so she was listening intently too, with her head in my lap.

I told them all about my encounters with the king and princess of Retice, as well as how I'd bumped into Lia briefly outside of the Great Labyrinth of Kantinen, and about Commander Saran's final moments. Though perhaps it wasn't right for me to call them his final moments, since he was already long dead by the time I got there.

"I see. Sounds like Retice is much worse off than I thought... That assassin team the king has on standby—the Night Ravens, was it?" Crow muttered something as a thought occurred to him. "Sounds like you owe Saran your life, then. He taught you everything you knew about this world, and he even helped you escape from the castle. He knew he'd be putting his life on the line to help you, but he did it anyway... Now, *that* sounds like the Saran I knew," Crow said with a snort. Crow had been so genuine with us lately that it was a relief to hear sarcasm. "Did you ever speak to the assassins, Akira?"

After thinking it through, I replied, "No. In fact, I don't think I ever even saw them. There was a group of soldiers I didn't recognize who tried to surround me when I escaped the castle, so it could have been them, but they also could have just been ordinary soldiers who I hadn't encountered before."

One would think a special team like the Night Ravens would have a uniform or some sort of identifying marker, but I never saw anything like that. Though it was possible they wanted to blend in, since no assassin worth his salt ever wanted to stand out from the crowd—especially if they were a member of a sup- posedly elite team.

"Well, it just so happens that I came across a rather interesting bit of information while I was digging up dirt on Gram," said Crow, looking up after a few moments of silence. His lips were curled into a smirk, and I was immediately intrigued. "Those strength-boosting drugs Gram loves to use? Let's call 'em 'boost- ers' for lack of a better word. Anyway, I found out two very inter- esting things about 'em—how they work, and where they've been exporting them to."

I wasn't sure what this had to do with the Retice assassins, but I kept listening.

"The boosters work by dramatically enhancing the combat abilities of the subject—whether they were originally a combat-oriented class or not—at the expense of turning them into mindless fighting machines. I still don't know if it takes more than a single dose to reach that point, or if they have to keep taking the drug to maintain the effect."

Amelia and I nodded to show we were still following, and Crow went on.

"At present, Gram's only been using the boosters on his beast-folk mercenaries, but it turns out they work on humans as well, and I found proof that a bulk quantity of the drug was exported to the Kingdom of Retice ten or so years ago. It was sent to an ordinary doctor, but that doctor just so happens to be one of the king's closest advisors these days."

So the king was the real *intended recipient, is what you're telling me.*

"Saran was so powerful that even the Demon Lord respected his strength. There's no way he could have been killed by ordinary humans easily, especially given that his light magic specialties lay in protection barriers and purification spells. An average assassination attempt via ambush or poisoning wouldn't have any hope of succeeding... No, these assassins must have been juiced beyond reason."

I bit my lip.

"So you're suggesting that these 'Night Ravens' were physically enhanced by the same boosters Gram uses on his mercenaries?" asked Amelia. "But wouldn't that make the king of Retice and Gram the *real* murderers of Saran Mithray, as the ones who created and gave orders to those killing machines?"

My eyes widened. I looked incredulously at Crow, who was watching me, amused.

"Is *this* why you've been doing so much intel gathering lately? You knew about all of this already, didn't you?" I demanded, but Crow simply shrugged his shoulders.

"I knew a little bit about you, yeah, but I had no idea you and Saran were pals. Honest. Pretty funny how all the loose ends sorta tied themselves together, huh?"

I scowled; I certainly didn't see the humor in it. Amelia, who was lost at this point, kept looking back and forth between me and Crow.

"Did you really think I wouldn't recognize the glint in your eyes as the look of a man who's hellbent on revenge? Me, the guy who's spent his whole life going after one man? Sorry, but I'm too old to play ignorant at this point," said Crow, his expression turning cold. "But we're here now. And it's time for you to get revenge for the both of us."

Amelia gasped and looked at me, finally realizing what was going on. "Akira... Are you telling me that in exchange for Crow being our guide on the demon continent, you're going to...?"

I didn't answer her unfinished question—I simply glared at Crow, who started laughing.

"That's right. That little 'favor' I asked of Akira was to assassinate Gram, and to exact revenge for my sister, since I'm too old and frail to do it myself anymore. But since Gram's also technically responsible for his beloved mentor's death, that just sweetens the deal, no? Not to mention, Gram's the one who made a deal with the demons to get them into the Great Labyrinth of Brute and kidnap Amelia."

Crow made eye contact with me, having forced me into silence. If I were the protagonist of a popular fantasy story, I would have been able to brush off everything Crow just said. To say revenge was pointless, and it was never what the deceased would have wanted. But I just couldn't do that. Because I wasn't the hero.

After traveling with Crow from Mali to Uruk, I'd learned he was really a good person deep down—he just had no people skills. I'd also learned that he was a good friend of Commander Saran's. I had seen the sort of pain and helplessness he lived with every day, wanting to avenge his sister but being physically incapable of doing so. After picking up on these things, I found it extremely hard to avert my eyes from his plight. Empathy could be a real pain sometimes.

Regardless, the information about the king of Retice using boosters from Gram to brainwash his assassins, and about Gram having brokered a deal with the demons who kidnapped Amelia— all of it was intel I'd received directly from Crow. I still had to do a little independent research of my own to verify these claims.

POV: NIGHT

"*U*GH, would it kill Master to not overwork his familiars?"
"Yeah, *or* his demons..."

There were few people out and about that night, and the streets were currently empty, save for a single prowling black cat and the person trailing him. Nights in Uruk were much quieter than in other major cities. While in most places, the lights would still be on and plenty of people would still be about, all the stores in Uruk closed quite early, and there were hardly any lights to speak of—not even streetlamps. This made the stars quite visible.

"I have to say, I wasn't expecting you to tag along, Lady Latticenail."

The Lady Latticenail I knew had always been an extremely self-minded princess, never following orders or hearing out requests. She spent each and every day trying to pull pranks on someone new, and she caused nothing but trouble for those around her. Her free-spirited nature caused His Majesty innumerable headaches, and not even Mahiro could thwart her mischievous designs.

"Hey, I'm just out here to have fun! Coming with you seemed like the most interesting thing to do today. Your master's pretty intriguing, though. You think he anticipated that I'd wanna tag along with you?"

I truly did not understand this girl. My entire life, I'd felt she and I simply did not mesh well, likely because I could not for the life of me wrap my head around the way she chose to conduct herself, let alone her way of thinking.

Her lavender eyes filled with glee as she scanned the surrounding area. "Okie-dokie, so next on our to-do list... He wanted us to find hard evidence to support the info we dug up, right?" she asked.

Resisting the urge to let out a heavy sigh, I nodded and tried to focus on the task at hand. *"Correct. We need to expose Guildmaster Gram's wrongdoing. Ideally by finding where they keep the drugs he's manufacturing and determining how and where they're being distributed."*

And if we could find evidence that they'd been shipped to the Kingdom of Retice, that would be even better... Honestly, where did Master get off making his familiar do all the footwork? If Lady Latticenail weren't here, it would be all but impossible for me to handle alone. Though maybe it was like she suggested, and he'd anticipated her coming along.

Our standard procedure thus far had been for Lady Latticenail to distract our targets (since her Mana Suppression Extra Skill made her indistinguishable from a human) while I snuck inside and gathered as much intel as I could find. In the event that I got caught, she could simply use her Mesmerize skill to smooth things over and make a clean getaway. She wasn't a huge fan of the plan, since she thought it made us no better than common burglars, but I needed her to get over it for Master's sake. It was, after all, the same exact method we'd used to gather intel back in Mali. I was hoping the same process would work equally well in Uruk, but it seemed the people of this city went to bed quite early, which would make it more difficult. The plan had been to arrive in Uruk with plenty of time to spare for investigating, but because Lady Latticenail kept getting sidetracked along the way, we hadn't made it until the sun had already set. How were we to fulfill Master's wishes now?

"Come now, my dear Night!" Latticenail said pompously.

I looked up to see her gazing at the Uruk Adventurer's Guild with an eerie glint in her eyes. What exactly did she have in mind?

"Are you quite prepared?"

"Um... Prepared for what, might I ask?"

Lady Latticenail suddenly grabbed me by the scruff of my neck and picked me up before dashing around the corner and into an alley behind the building.

"Okay, have a nice flight!" she said, then flung me into the air.

"H-have you lost your MIIIND?!" I screamed as I careened upward before landing on the rooftop. I knew screaming was a surefire way to get us caught, but she hadn't left me much of a choice, slinging me to the roof without so much as a word of warning. I looked down over the eaves to give the perpetrator a piece of my mind, only to find her smiling sheepishly.

"What in the world *were you—"* I started, but then I realized she wasn't looking at me. She was looking at the mouth of the alley.

"Hey! What the hell do you think you're doing here at this hour, little girl?!"

As a bunch of light sources flooded into the alleyway, I saw that Latticenail was completely surrounded by city guards, but she didn't seem fazed by the intimidating soldiers in the slightest and just kept on smiling.

"Oh, well, y'see, I'm just a simple traveler, and this is my first night in town. But before I could even find an inn to stay at, everyone suddenly disappeared! Looks like I'm gonna have to

sleep outside tonight! But I guess I got a little lost, tee hee. Could one of you big, strong guards lead me out to the city gates? Heck, I don't even know where we are right now!"

I was surprised at how quickly she'd thought up a story, especially given how much she vehemently hated liars. Even if it was for the purposes of avoiding a fight with the city guards, I never thought she'd lie. Everything was riding on her story, and one little slip-up could mean curtains for us.

"Whaddya mean, kid? We're in the alley behind the Adventurer's Guild—it's about as far from the city gates as you can get. And didn't anyone ever tell you it's dangerous to go wandering in this city without a guide?"

"No way! Seriously?! Gosh, I guess my sense of direction's even worse than I thought! Oopsie, tee hee!"

Apparently, this wasn't an uncommon occurrence, and the guards quickly walked off with Lady Latticenail in tow. As soon as they took their eyes off her, she looked up at me and gave a little wink to wish me luck. I nodded back, then snuck in through the (thankfully) unlocked skylight.

When it came to sensitive information, most people kept it somewhere it wouldn't accidentally be discovered. The attic I landed in fit the bill. At first glance, the only things that seemed to be stored in the attic were a broken broom and a bunch of trash, but it was still worth taking a look. Gram didn't seem like the type to go to great lengths to destroy the evidence, so it was entirely possible that I'd find something damning without much trouble.

Being in cat form was awfully convenient when searching for hidden things—I could sneak into tight spaces, and with great olfactory senses, I could easily sniff things out. For *really* tight spaces, I would probably need to shapeshift into a slime, but I really didn't want to do that unless absolutely necessary. Using Shapeshifter cost an enormous amount of mana, and all the slimes I'd encountered that I could turn into were bright and gaudy colors, hardly good for stealth; I hadn't personally seen the black slime that Lady Amelia described, thus that color wasn't an option. And while a dog might have had a better sense of smell than a cat, I had a predisposition against canines and preferred to avoid them whenever possible.

"Doesn't seem like anyone's been in here for quite some time. I'm not catching a whiff of any scents, unfortunately."

The room hadn't been cleaned in quite some time, so the entire place was caked in a thick layer of dust. It seemed safe to assume there probably wasn't anything mission-critical hidden up here, but just as I was searching for a ladder leading down-stairs, a corner of the floor opened up. I hid under a nearby desk. Presumably, this was the door to the attic I'd been looking for, and someone had just opened it from down below.

"Ugh. Why do I gotta climb up into this musty old attic just to hide *his* dirty laundry?" I heard someone mutter as they clam-bered up the ladder. "I get that I'm basically a slave to him, but would it kill him to take care of this junk himself? Like, what would he do if I did a crappy job of hiding it and someone else found it? I dunno what the king was thinking, making a guy like that guildmaster... Though it's not like King Dingaling's all that great at his job either."

I held my breath as though my life depended on it, but thankfully, the grumbling man never came anywhere near the desk I was hiding beneath.

"Lord knows the world would be a better place without 'em... Both Gram *and* the king."

I could only assume he was talking about King Igsam (whom Master had met earlier today), but I was struggling to imagine what sort of person he must be for his citizens to loathe him so much. I doubted this disgruntled man was the only one who referred to him as "King Dingaling."

"Why doesn't he just burn these documents, anyway? All they are is a potential liability for him."

The man grumbled and complained but still did as he'd been told, which I was very grateful for. If what he claimed was accurate, then these documents were exactly the type of evidence Master was looking for.

After a moment, the man left the attic.

"This was the easiest stakeout yet!"

Everything Crow had said was true. Gram had bought a human woman with a chemist class as a slave and forced her to create the boosters for him. Her name was Amaryllis Cluster. She had won the Mali beauty pageant a few years back, and she'd been sold shortly after. I didn't want to believe the rumors of a burgeoning slave trade in beastfolk territory, but I couldn't argue with facts. I knew Lady Amelia had been pursued by organ traffickers, but if the common folk were to learn that the royal family was involved in slavery, respect for the crown would crash to an all-time low.

"All right, now I just have to bring this paperwork back to Master, and I can finally be by his side again."

Since the pageant in Mali, Master and I had only communicated telepathically, so we hadn't actually met face-to-face in quite a while. I folded up the documents detailing Gram's misdeeds and held them in my mouth as I exited through the skylight. It didn't feel like I'd been in the attic for very long, yet the sky was already lightening. Once morning came, I'd need to use Telepathy to ask Master which inn they were staying at, but before that, I needed to regroup with Lady Latticenail.

"Hey, you made it out alive! Nice work!"

I sought out the highest hill on the outskirts of town, and sure enough, that was where I found Lady Latticenail. Whenever she ran and hid from us back at the Demon Lord's castle, she'd always go somewhere up high—and as His Majesty always said, "Where smoke will rise, fools will climb." I didn't quite understand his meaning, but it always managed to make Lady Latticenail puff out her cheeks in displeasure, so I assumed it was an insult.

"So how'd it go?" she asked.

"Quite well. Look here—written evidence showing Gram not only owns slaves and forces them to make illegal drugs, but also exports them to the human continent!"

Lady Latticenail's eyes went wide as she scanned the papers I'd found. "Where in the world did you find this stuff?"

"Erm, up in the attic of that building you threw me on top of. Why do you ask?" I said.

She narrowed her eyes for a split second before resuming her usual smile. "Well, that's great news."

"Indeed. Thank you very much for your assistance, Lady Latticenail. I do feel bad for making you lie, however..."

"What? I didn't lie. You know how much I hate liars, don't you?" she said, genuine confusion on her face.

"B-but when those soldiers surrounded you, you said..."

"All I said was that I was a traveler who was new in town, and that everyone was already off the streets by the time I got here, which is true. As was me saying I was gonna have to sleep outside for the night, and that I didn't know where I was. After all, all I did was follow you the whole time, don'tcha remember? I wasn't paying any attention to where we were walking. I didn't tell a single lie."

"A-as if! How else would you have known which roof to throw me on top of?!"

"Oh, yeah, that..." She flashed a devilish grin. "Guess I just happened to throw you in the right direction and you just happened to land on the roof of the Adventurer's Guild, which had an unlocked skylight leading into the attic where someone just happened to leave the evidence we were looking for, huh?"

Her mischievous smirk was beginning to creep me out, so I took a step backward, but this only made her grin wider.

"Don't sweat the small stuff, big guy. Sometimes coincidences happen, and you need to embrace that... Now your master gets what he wants, and I got to have a fun little time too. All's well that ends well!"

I feared I would never understand this girl. Unlike Master, who had a clear goal in mind at all times—returning home—I had no idea where Latticenail's motivations lay, nor what purpose she was living her life in pursuit of. And I found that genuinely terrifying.

POV: ODA AKIRA

EARLY THE NEXT MORNING, I got a telepathic transmission from Night asking where we were staying, and only a few minutes after I told him, he and Latticenail arrived at our hotel room door. The sun wasn't fully up yet, so Amelia and Crow were still fast asleep in the room next door.

"Here is what you requested, Master."

I grabbed the documents from Night's mouth and gave him some pets and chin scritches as a reward, and he started purring loudly. "Thanks, this is huge. And thanks to you too, Latticenail."

Latticenail smiled and stuck her head out toward me.

Confused, I tilted my head. "What are you doing?" I asked.

She turned her eyes up at me and pouted. "Ugh! I'm sayin' I want head pats too, numbnuts! How come you recognize when *she* wants 'em, but not me?"

"Because Amelia's the only woman whose body language I care to understand—ever think of that? And no, I will not be giving you any head pats." I was so confused; why was this demon acting so entitled?

She let out a heavy sigh and gazed upward. "Sheesh, I got first place in that beauty pageant too, y'know. Way to make me lose confidence in myself."

Personally, I was convinced she'd only won by a fluke—something about the lighting must have shown her off at the perfect angle or something. Growing tired of dealing with Latticenail, I shook my head and turned to Night, who had been watching her with a pensive look.

"What's the matter?" I asked, scooping him up in my arm, and he looked at the documents in my other hand. *Right, I still need to take a look at those. Whoops. I blame Latticenail for distracting me.* I unfolded the sheets of paper and gave them a quick once-over, and then I understood why Night was so on edge. "Night, where exactly did you find this stuff?"

"In the attic of the Adventurer's Guild," Night replied with a puzzled look. *"Why do you ask? Lady Latticenail asked the same thing. Is something strange about those documents? Are they forgeries?"*

I gave him some pets to reassure him, and he purred loudly once more.

"No, it's not that. It's just that they're almost *too* perfect, is all. But I'm pretty sure all the info written there is legit," said Latticenail.

But therein lies the problem.

"Thing is, if these were really just lying around in the attic of the Adventurer's Guild, then that probably means there's someone else out to assassinate Gram. Someone who's much closer to him than he even realizes, most likely."

I nodded in agreement. If we didn't act fast, someone might steal this hit job right out from under our noses.

"W-wait a minute! How can you know that for certain just based on where the documents were hidden? Couldn't it just as easily have been an oversight on Gram's part?"

"I mean, look at this. Doesn't it seem a little funny to you?" I said, holding the papers out in front of Night. I felt kind of bad that he was still having trouble seeing what the problem was, so I decided to lay it out for him (though I couldn't resist a little chuckle). "First off, why would anyone keep a neat and tidy list summarizing all of their crimes up in their attic? What would the point be? I mean, look at this stuff... Human trafficking, organ trafficking, murders, the names of all the mercenaries under his employ. It's almost like these documents were prepared specifically to tell someone like us about Gram's crimes. Hell, you could probably start a war with something like this. Slavery's totally illegal among the beastfolk nations, after all. Even assuming someone close to Gram was instructed to hide these somewhere no one could find them, they clearly did it in a way that suggests they *wanted* them to be stolen, or maybe that there was someone *else* who was supposed to come pick them up. You just beat them to the punch."

Now that Night had a handle on the implications of all of this, his expression grew grim. *"It wouldn't just lead to war. It would mean the utter dismantling of the royal family of Uruk. And if that were to happen, Lady Lia's life would be in danger too."*

Of course it would lead to a revolt. Just the word *slavery* was enough to fill any beastfolk with disgust, so the idea of a royal family member doing it? And according to these documents, it wasn't just beastfolk slaves, but humans and elves too. Some of these names were probably those of the elven wives and children I'd sworn to save. I couldn't exactly turn a blind eye now, when I'd stumbled upon where they were being held.

"To be honest with you, I really couldn't care less whether this or any country in this world falls apart," I said. "However..."

Now that we'd stuck our heads into this conspiracy, it felt like we had a responsibility to do whatever we could to stop it. I wasn't sure how much I could do to protect Lia's family, realistically, but she *had* cast that barrier that saved our hides down in the Great Labyrinth of Brute, and she'd helped us out of a bind yesterday. Not to mention, Amelia had taken a real liking to her. I let out a heavy sigh. The only thing these documents didn't tell us was who had been meant to find them.

"It's the Kingdom of Retice," said a voice from the next room. I turned to see Crow standing in the doorway. How did he always know exactly when to make the perfect entrance? It was starting to really freak me out. Only this time, I was less surprised by what he had to say and more repulsed.

"The Kingdom of Retice? What about it?"

That was the country that had summoned us to do its bidding, and the one that had killed Commander Saran. If I hadn't run away when I did, I would probably be pushing up daisies right next to Commander Saran. There was no doubt in my mind they'd summoned us for nefarious purposes, and if it weren't for my classmates still stuck there, I would be happy to never hear the name "Retice" ever again.

"I heard the gist of your conversation, and I think your supposition is mostly correct. Think about it: What country would benefit the most from having documents that would give them an excuse to go to war...? If you ask me, it can only be Retice," Crow said as he trotted into my room and plopped down on the sofa.

"I'll go ahead and refrain from asking what the hell a demon's doing in our hotel room," Crow went on, looking suspiciously at Latticenail, who shivered uncomfortably in response. Since Crow didn't have World Eyes, he shouldn't have been able to see through her Mana Suppression skill and recognize her as a demon. He must have known her, but he continued speaking before I had a chance to ask. "Anyway, you wanna know how things are going over in the Kingdom of Retice right now? You've got a lot of acquaintances over there, don't you?"

"More like comrades, but yeah," I said. They were more than acquaintances, but certainly not friends. It was hard to express the concept of "classmates" in a world where that term didn't exist. Hell, I wasn't even sure they had schools. "To be honest, I couldn't care less what becomes of them, though I suppose I might lose a little sleep if they were to die due to my own inaction."

"Gotcha... Well, I'm afraid I don't have any intel to share about the other summoned heroes. All I can say is that the amount of food being shipped into the castle hasn't changed."

I was surprised to hear myself sigh in relief—apparently, I cared more about my classmates than I thought. I didn't regret running away from the castle the day they tried to pin the commander's murder on me, but I did wish I could have done something to break all my classmates free of the curse they were under beforehand. I'd been too caught up in my own business and still reeling from Commander Saran's death. I liked to tell myself they'd be safe so long as Gilles was there to look after them, but now he had left the castle behind, and I could only speculate as to how they were doing now. I didn't know why the hero and his party had left the others behind, but I could assume the vast majority still hated my guts.

"As long as they're not dead, I guess. Anything else you'd like to share? I assume you've got good reason to believe the kingdom's trying to start a war?" I asked, and Crow gave a solemn nod, his expression grim.

"I do," he replied. "When you were back at the castle, did you ever hear rumors circulating about how the king had taken an interest in the art of resurrecting the dead?"

I searched my memory, then nodded. I recalled Commander Saran telling me something along those lines in the castle archives. About how the king had lost his beloved wife in a tragic accident, and how he'd devoted his life to bringing her back, even at the expense of completely neglecting their daughter. I had to wonder if the same sort of obsession would consume me were I to lose my mom or my sister.

I had shrugged off the story when I first heard it because I was under the impression it was impossible to bring back the dead, even in a world with magic. Hell, even with Amelia's Resurrection Magic, it wasn't possible to bring back people who'd been dead for decades. Things like that only happened in fairy tales.

"But what does it matter?" I asked. "It's not possible, and I don't see what that could have to do with them trying to pick a fight with Uruk." If bringing people back from the dead was possible, then we wouldn't need to go on this dangerous revenge quest to begin with.

Crow's face remained deadly serious. "What if I told you it *was* possible, at least theoretically?" he asked, and I could almost feel the blood of everyone in the room run cold.

"Oh, come now, surely you jest? One can't simply bring back the dead," Night muttered incredulously.

But Crow wasn't the type to say something like that lightly, and if it was true, then there was a chance we could bring his sister back.

"Hate to break it to you, but you actually can... Only problem is it costs tens, or even hundreds of thousands of lives in exchange. Not sure *I* know anyone who'd want to come back from the dead if they knew it meant sacrificing that many innocent people, but hey, to each their own."

I was taken aback by this information, but also a little relieved to hear Crow had no delusions of attempting something like that to bring back his sister.

"How does it even work? And why does it cost such an exorbitant amount of lives just to bring back one person?" I asked.

"I couldn't tell you; all I know is the price for bringing one person back to life via the Equivalent Exchange skill is an ungodly amount of lives. Hence why the king of Retice is itching to start a war. At first, he was trying to pick a fight with the human nation of Yamato, but Gilles and company put a stop to that."

I see. That would explain why he had been forced to resign from his post. I didn't know which country was stronger, but a war between them would have certainly resulted in countless deaths. I wondered if the people of Retice were in support of this warmongering, or if the king was just too cruel to care what they had to say.

In any case, this Equivalent Exchange skill seemed like quite the game-changer. From the way Crow made it sound, it was capable of letting someone do just about anything they pleased, so long as they could pay the necessary price. Such a skill would be invaluable not just in combat scenarios, but for everyday purposes as well.

"And how exactly did you come into possession of this intel?" I asked, finally giving voice to the biggest question I'd wanted to ask. Where in the hell was Crow getting all this precious information from?

Crow simply laughed and tousled my hair. "That's a secret," he said before waltzing out of the room.

God, why did he have to act like such a typical overconfident pretty-boy? Especially when he was old enough to be in a nursing home.

"Okay, folks! Today, we're gonna make up for the guided city tour I didn't have the chance to give you yesterday!"

After the sun had fully risen, and Amelia was drowsily eating her breakfast, Lia paid a visit to our hotel room. When Amelia had first woken up and seen Latticenail and Night hanging out, she'd stood there dumbfounded for a minute before gleefully embracing them both as I explained the task I'd asked them to perform. Amelia had not seen Night in weeks, after all.

Given that we hadn't given Lia our hotel information, Crow must've told her. As I watched Lia and Crow converse happily with each other, I couldn't help but wonder at the relationship dynamic between them. It remained a mystery to me.

With Night on my shoulders for the first time in ages, we stepped out into the city. Latticenail decided to tag along, albeit with her face concealed under her hood. Beastfolk had awfully good noses, so there was a chance they'd be able to sniff her out as a demon even with her Mana Suppression skill on. How they could possibly recognize the scent of demon, I didn't know, but it was better to be safe than sorry, especially considering that if anyone were to discover her identity, there'd be nothing but trouble. Latticenail herself was initially opposed to the idea, but she eventually caved to reason, donning the monster-repelling cloak Mahiro had made (which could also conceal her presence).

"Glad you decided to come along today, Crow!" Lia said happily.

"Yeah," said Crow, who was walking beside her.

Lia seemed to be feeling a lot more chipper today, at least judging by her tail swinging rapidly to and fro. I remembered hearing that dogs wagged their tails when they were in a good mood... Or was that an indicator that they liked someone? I forgot. In any case, Lia seemed to be really enjoying herself today.

"*Someone* sure looks happy," Amelia remarked as she watched the two of them.

"She must've really been looking forward to seeing Crow, eh?" Latticenail teased.

Night and I looked at each other, neither of us quite understanding what they were getting at. The two women sighed as though we were the most hopeless men on the planet.

"Can't you guys tell? Lia's totally got a thing for Crow. As in, a *crush* kind of thing. Anyone with eyeballs can see it."

I stopped dead in my tracks. Night looked just as shocked as I did.

"God, guys are so dense about this sort of thing. I literally just met the girl this morning, and even I could tell." Latticenail sighed.

In my defense, today was the first time I'd seen the two of them interact. But if she *did* have a crush on him, that would explain why she seemed weirdly jealous that Amelia had learned Inversion from him before she did.

"Okay, I'll admit I didn't realize it, but isn't the age gap between them a little *too* wide?" I wondered aloud. After all, Crow had to be at least a hundred years older than her.

"Oh, age doesn't matter one bit in beastfolk relationships! Especially since beastfolk don't generally show the physical effects of aging. Hence why most people wouldn't really bat an eye to find out that a youngster like Lia was dating a geezer like Crow. Y'know, hypothetically."

I had to admit, the words coming out of Latticenail's mouth were giving me serious culture shock, but I tried to wrap my head around it as I looked up at Lia, who was blushing from ear to ear. This was unmistakably the face of a girl in love. Then again, I felt like I'd seen Yui make faces like that whenever Kyousuke was around, so maybe not.

"Let's give the two of them some alone time, shall we?" Amelia suggested.

"Yeah, good idea," Latticenail said, and the two of them turned down a nearby side street.

Figuring Crow would be able to sense we'd taken a different route, I decided to follow after them.

"Wait a minute. Isn't this the street where...?"

As we turned the corner, Night started looking around nervously. Latticenail, too, narrowed her lavender eyes upon noticing a particular signboard.

"Yeah, we came through here last night. Which means if we follow this road all the way, it'll take us straight to the Adventurer's Guild."

It was off the main road, yet plenty of people were still using the side street—many of them clearly adventurers, and many more than even in Ur.

"Would you like to stop by the Guild, Akira?"

Come to think of it, I hadn't been to a Guild branch since we left Ur. I had no reason to, especially since Crow had been ensuring we didn't have to pay for our hotels, but I *was* interested to see what the largest Guild branch in the beastfolk kingdoms looked like. Especially since Gram was the guildmaster of said branch.

"Sure, why not? I'm curious as to what it's like."

"Then let's head on over there!" Latticenail said, taking the lead. I asked if she knew the way, and she said she never forgot a path once tread. I liked to think I had a pretty good memory for those sorts of things too, but the labyrinth that was Uruk city had made me reconsider. "This was the place, right kitty-cat?"

"Yes, this is the one."

It was a fairly dingy looking building from the outside, featuring the same crossed swords emblem painted on a sign outside the Ur branch. Presumably, it was the emblem of the Adventurer's Guild.

"I'll wait outside. Just holler at me when you're done! I might be behind the building," said Latticenail.

"Got it. Will do. Well then, shall we?"

I watched Latticenail turn the corner, then placed my hand on the door to the Adventurer's Guild and stepped inside.

My Status as an
Assassin Obviously
Exceeds the Hero's

✦ CHAPTER 5 ✦

A Chance Encounter

POV: ODA AKIRA

THE UR BRANCH of the Adventurer's Guild had been fairly clean and presentable for what was ultimately a glorified tavern. The Uruk branch, by contrast, was a dismal, gloomy place. Dark red stains covered the walls, which told me fights within these walls weren't an unusual occurrence. It was in every way how I'd originally imagined an establishment like this would be, in the worst possible sense. Perhaps the guildmaster's personality was rubbing off on the Guild members—or I was just overthinking it.

There was a large counter at the far end of the building with employees running around busily behind it. There were fewer employees than at the Ur branch, and most notably, there were no requests posted on the walls. I could only assume the people behind the counter handled all of the purchasing of monster parts, acceptance and doling out of requests, and rank decisions. It was an inefficient way of doing things, almost to the point of being ridiculous.

The Guild members, meanwhile, were taking a load off and enjoying a nice drink. This was the same in every city—plenty of adventurers would wake up bright and early just to drink the whole day away. When I entered the building, their gazes landed on me first, before moving to Amelia, and then finally to Night. Staring happened all the time, so I was mostly used to it.

"Welcome to the Adventurer's Guild of Uruk. What business might you have with us today?" asked a pale-faced employee who'd dashed out from behind the counter to greet us the moment he saw Amelia's face. She had become something of a recognizable celebrity after winning the beauty pageant, which meant she got a lot of unwanted looks. They didn't bother her anywhere near as much as they bothered me.

"Yo, ain't that Princess Amelia...?"

"Thought I heard that pageant winners always disappear."

"Sure she's not an impostor?"

The gallery of drunkards was giving free live commentary loud enough for us to hear. Why did drunks always have to be so boorish? Why couldn't they just drown their sorrows in peace? I assumed the only reason they weren't bad-mouthing Night was that they couldn't see him.

"And that guy in the black, is he supposed to be her body-guard? Guy looks weak as hell. If he tried to block one of my attacks, he'd get blown all the way to kingdom come," grumbled a red-haired man sitting a short distance away.

Amelia twitched angrily—the quip had evidently offended her, even though I'd just shrugged it off. She was supposed to be talking to the Guild employee, yet her gaze was fixed on the redheaded guy.

"We're not here on any business. We were simply passing by and wanted to see what sort of place the Guild branch of the largest beastfolk kingdom was. Yet it seems the adventurers you have here are nothing more than a bunch of cowards. Don't you all have something better to do than drinking and bickering in here morning, noon, and night?"

Whenever Amelia got like this, her glare became so ice-cold that it really felt as though she'd brought the temperature down. It was something only she could do, and the Guild employee who'd approached us squealed in fright before taking a step back.

"Beg your pardon?! Who you callin' a coward, little girl?! I'm a silver-rank adventurer—Raúl the Whirlwind! Maybe you've heard of me?!"

The only thing I wanted to say to the large lionman who'd just kicked over his chair in protest was *So what?* Judging by the way Amelia narrowed her frigid eyes, I knew she was thinking the same thing.

"And? You think any silver-rank adventurer with a nickname deserves unconditional respect? You think you just get to say and do whatever you like? Get over yourself, you pathetic child," Amelia scoffed. The chill that fell over the building was honestly a bit terrifying. If I were in this adventurer's shoes right now, I'd get on my knees and beg for mercy, but apparently, he felt differently.

"Shut up, shut up, shut up!" the lionman cried like the pathetic child she'd accused him of being, then raised his fists to take a swing at her. His fellow adventurers tried to tell him to stop, but he would not be deterred.

"Sorry, can't let you do that, bud," I said, wrapping one arm around Amelia and blocking his fist with the other. So much for sending me flying to kingdom come—his wimpy punch didn't move me even a little. It felt like being slapped by a baby. I was having a hard time believing this Raúl guy was an adventurer at all.

"Amelia, that was uncalled for," I chided her, and then turned to look the man in the eye. "We're sorry for causing a commotion, but I would suggest you watch your mouth unless you feel like losing your head today. This is a genuine elven princess you're talking to."

Upon hearing my warning, the drunkards seemed to realize what they'd done, and they went pale. The Guild employees who'd been suspicious of Amelia averted their eyes.

"All right, douchebag! Now let go of my freakin' hand!" roared the lionman, his beady golden eyes glaring down at me; I preferred Night's golden eyes, personally.

"Yeah, not gonna happen. The moment I let go, you might just try to take another swing at me. In the future, I'd suggest not attacking strangers when you don't have the slightest clue how powerful they might be. And didn't your mother ever teach you to treat other people's property with respect?" I said, looking at the chair he'd kicked over.

Raúl wasn't listening to any of this, however, and just kept trying to pull his hand free. But I wouldn't let go. "You made your point; now let go of me already!"

I didn't know whether he'd understood my point, but I decided to be nice and let go of his hand.

"Sorry about that!" said a young human girl who wheeled herself out from behind the counter in a device akin to a wheelchair. She had bright, golden-yellow hair, and she lowered her head to us in apology. "Raúl's kind of a dunderhead, so he couldn't judge an opponent's strength even if his life depended on it!"

"What the—?! Hey! Kerria! Who you callin' a dunderhead?!" yelled Raúl, approaching the girl.

"The same man who keeps trying to pick fights he can't win and never learns his lesson!" Kerria yelled back, puffing out her cheeks and clenching her fists.

"Ha ha, there they go again..."

"It's like an everyday thing with them..."

The mood in the building relaxed a little as the other adventurers cracked jokes at this seemingly standard exchange.

"Anyway, I'm really sorry for the trouble! If you want to decapitate Raúl, feel free, but please don't think worse of the Adventurer's Guild for his behavior!" she said, bowing again.

"Hey! Don't throw me under the bus!" he whined.

It seemed the incident had sobered up the drunkards who'd been badmouthing us earlier, and they promptly filed out of the building with pale faces. Kerria gestured toward an open table, and we sat down, still chuckling about their dispute. The other Guild employees looked on and laughed too, not even attempting to step in and put a stop to it. None of the beastfolk in the building seemed to be afraid of Night either—he was lying still on my shoulders in an attempt to look docile, like a little plushie. I could tell he was trying not to laugh.

"I don't think less of any of you or the Adventurer's Guild, don't worry," said Amelia, now calming down after her hearty laugh. "If anything, I was the one who was out of line. I apologize," she said, bowing her head.

"Oh, no, please! Anyone with eyes could see it was all Raúl's fault! Raúl, apologize to the nice lady!" said Kerria.

Raúl, for his part, had turned away and was pouting like a child. Kerria reached up and forced him to lower his head to us with a level of force I found difficult to believe possible from those pale, slender arms. Was she truly just a human? I even used World Eyes to check her stats because I was genuinely suspicious, but she really was just an ordinary girl.

"Ow, hey! What the hell, Kerria?!"

"None of this would have happened if it weren't for that big mouth of yours! And don't take potshots at people who are only calling you what you are! You promised you'd stop pulling this nonsense! I'm gonna ban you from the premises!"

I was beginning to wonder when this would end. I'd never seen a couple argue quite as much as these two did, yet it seemed like their relationship was more than resilient enough to handle it.

"Could you two please stop making a spectacle? You're embarrassing us in front of our esteemed guests," said a man in an indigo kimono with narrow, discerning eyes.

"Oh, God! M-my apologies, sir!" said Kerria, flustered, and

she and Kerria finally ceased their bickering. I smiled awkwardly and waved my hands to indicate I wasn't offended.

"It's a pleasure to meet you, Princess Amelia. And you as well, Mr. 'Silent Assassin,'" the man said. "My name is Mamoru, and I am the assistant guildmaster of this humble establishment. I've heard quite a few stories about the two of you."

Ugh. I hate that stupid nickname. What assassin gets recognized on sight like a celebrity?

The man had a very Japanese-sounding name and wore Japanese-style garb, so I could only assume he'd come from the human nation of Yamato.

"My, my. I must say, I've never seen anyone with such deep 'ring' marks as the two of you," Mamoru commented, looking down at the matching scars on my and Amelia's fingers.

"What, you guys know about the ring thing here too?" I asked.

"Oh, yes. But few will actually scar themselves like you two have—most simply put a little iron ring around their fingers. It's a very popular practice among adventurer couples. It serves as an ever-present reminder of their eternal love in a profession where death could always be just one mistake away."

Amelia cocked her head to one side, indicating to me that she'd heard something else. "Lia told me lots of people in the palace do the scar thing," she said.

"Well, there are a lot of adulterous love affairs that happen within the walls of that palace. My guess would be they're just thin scrapes and markings meant to keep them out of trouble. They can be erased at any time. But with scars as deep as yours, you'd need some very powerful recovery magic in order to make them vanish without a trace."

Aha. So it served as cheating prevention matter, then—kept both parties honest. This was news to me.

"In any case, I can assure you these two are no impostors, Raúl," said Mamoru, trying to convince him.

But the lionman just stood there speechless, as if in a daze. "Are you really the Silent Assassin?" he asked incredulously.

I felt a bit discombobulated, unable to reconcile this calm behavior with his childish temper tantrum, but nodded nonetheless. "I really don't like that nickname, but yeah, that's me."

Raúl dropped to the floor and prostrated himself in front of me. He was doing such a good job of it that he might very well put most Japanese people to shame. I had to wonder where he'd learned the gesture.

"Oh, please forgive me!"

"Uh, what?" I blurted, unable to process this sudden turn of events. Thankfully, Kerria swooped in to explain.

"Truth is, Raúl here's a huge fan of the Silent Assassin. He was in Ur when the demon invasion happened, and he saw you take out all those monsters in one fell swoop from a distance..."

I found it hard to see how anything I had done that day would be something to fanboy about. All I did was lose control of my shadows in fury after hearing Amelia had been kidnapped, and then they swallowed up those monsters in an instant. If anything, it seemed like something people would fear me for, not celebrate.

The old me, certainly, would have had nightmares after seeing something like that.

"Ever since, whenever he sees someone dressed even somewhat similar to the Silent Assassin he blows his top and tries to pick fights with 'em... He's a dunderhead, so he never once considered the possibility that his idol would come here."

What the hell? How does someone even get like that? I was at a loss for words. I mean, to be fair, an assassin *shouldn't* go walking around in broad daylight for all to see, but that didn't mean Raúl should try to beat up everyone dressed in all black. That sounded like the sort of fan I wanted nothing to do with.

"Er... Can you really call yourself a fan if you want to beat up everyone else who dresses like me?" I asked, as he hung his head in shame.

"Well, 'cause they were tryin' to act like you and stuff, and it pissed me off," he grumbled. "I know it was wrong."

I was beginning to feel like an interrogator. I genuinely couldn't say if this man had a flawed way of thinking or he just didn't think things through. In any event, I'd learned from his interactions with Kerria that he wasn't the sort of person who learned his lesson from sternly worded lectures.

"Well, just make sure it doesn't happen again. And lift that head up already."

"Yessir!" he replied happily, lifting his head as instructed. His eyes were twinkling like a dog awaiting a treat.

POV: LIA LAGOON

"SHEESH, so much for giving them a guided tour of the city..." I muttered.

I was a little miffed that the three people (and a cat) walking behind us had disappeared without me noticing—and while I didn't know when exactly they'd left, I assumed it was probably a good while ago. I was a failure as a tour guide.

"Did *you* notice they were gone, Lord Crow?"

"Of course I did. Who do you think I am?" he responded as though it were the dumbest question in the world, and for the first time, I was angry with him.

I puffed out my cheeks and glared. "Then why didn't you stop them or tell me?!"

"You're the guide here, not me. It's your fault for getting too caught up in our conversation... On another note, could you stop calling me 'Lord Crow'?"

Sudden topic change aside, I couldn't help but be confused. I didn't see anything wrong with the honorific. Crow, however, sighed at my reaction. I had called him simply "Crow" long ago, before I knew anything about him, but it felt almost sacrilegious to call a member of the legendary hero's party by his first name alone.

Crow, perhaps reading my thoughts, narrowed his eyes and looked down at me. "Tell me: What kind of relationship do we have, you and I?"

"Uhhh... Well, you gave me my name, so I guess you're like my godfather, and that makes me your godchild?"

I learned at a young age it hadn't been my parents who named me, but Lord Crow. I didn't know why he'd chosen the name he did, other than that it was part of the name of someone he respected. To this day, I still didn't know who that was. I didn't realize what an honor it was to be named by him until I was older.

"In what universe does a godchild call their godparent 'Lord'?" he teased.

"This one, apparently," I mumbled, and he stared daggers at me. I remembered him glaring at me like this many times in the past—the only difference now was that I was taller and his glare was closer, so his frustration was all the more palpable. I wondered why I never felt afraid of these eyes as a child. I stared long into his unfathomably deep blue eyes, but Crow quickly got embarrassed and looked away.

"Whatever. Let's get out of here, shall we? Feels pretty awkward being here."

I looked around, and my cheeks went bright red. We were standing in one of the most popular make-out spots in the city (which I had originally included in the tour after receiving confirmation from Lady Amelia yesterday that she and Akira were indeed in love). The entire area was filled with couples unashamed to be—and maybe even enjoying—making out in public. "Awkward" did not even begin to describe it.

"M-my apologies! Let's head somewhere else, right away!"

I grabbed Lord Crow by the hand and dashed away from the make-out spot. After running to the next street over, I finally stopped to catch my breath.

"Pff... Pfft... Ha ha ha!"

Before I could even do that, I heard Lord Crow cackling un-controllably behind me. This man, who almost never cracked a smile, was now clutching his sides and doing everything he could to hold in his laughter.

"L-Lord Crow?!"

Were it anyone else, I would have been cracking up right alongside them, but Lord Crow was different. Even during fes-tivals and other times of merriment, when everyone and their mother was laughing nonstop, this man had always remained stone-faced, never even flinching. Had he come down with something, or what?

"You really are funny, you know that?" he said with a smile before placing a hand on my head. I looked up (he was still a fair bit taller than me, after all) at what could very well have been the first true smile I'd ever seen on his face. As he ruffled my hair, I froze. I could feel a flush coming over me, the likes of which I'd never felt before.

"Wha... No, I... Huh?"

I wanted to ask what the heck he was doing, but the words caught in my throat, and only confused little fragments leaked out from my incredulous mouth. I still couldn't believe Lord Crow was single—he'd been a bachelor his whole life. It wasn't like he was unattractive. If it weren't for the sour look on his face all the time, he could have at least had a wife or two over the years. It was an incredible thing to see a man like that smiling and enjoying the company of a member of the opposite sex.

"Hello? You all right down there?" he asked.

Snapping back to my senses, I found Lord Crow with his usual blank expression back in place and his hand already back down by his side. I bobbed my head to assure him I was fine, and he accepted the gesture before walking off. I trotted along after him, wondering if I'd dreamed that little interaction. Then I caught the slightest hint of a smile on Lord Crow's lips.

"It wasn't a dream..." I whispered.

"You say something?" Lord Crow asked, looking down at me.

"No, nothing at all!" I shook my head profusely. "Er, anyway, where are we going?"

He was walking with purpose as opposed to just traipsing around the city to kill time, and even though this was the city I called home, it was designed like a labyrinth, so I couldn't guess where we might be headed.

"I'll tell you when we get there."

"But then we'll already be there! What's the point of telling me after I already know?!"

Lord Crow did not acknowledge my extremely compelling argument.

Right, left, right, right... We'd taken so many turns, I was having trouble keeping track. All I knew was that Lord Crow had taken us far away from the main drag. At first, I'd been trying to guess where we might be headed, but we were walking on streets I'd never seen before in my entire life, so I'd thrown my hands up in defeat. The city was much too convoluted for even its residents to get a handle on. The street we were on right now was so remote and gloomy, I wasn't even sure what part of the city we were in. All I knew was that my feet hurt like crazy from all the walking.

"How much longer until we get there?" I asked for the umpteenth time. Lord Crow's unrelenting pace told me we weren't lost, but I felt a little uneasy walking around unfamiliar territory.

"Should only be a few more minutes... Why? Your poor little legs about to give out 'cause you've gotten too used to the pampered princess lifestyle?"

I knew he was trying to get a rise out of me, but I frowned nonetheless. "My legs are just fine, thank you very much! Look, it's not *my* fault I'm nervous when you refuse to tell me where the heck we're even going!"

"Oh, do you get nervous walking through unfamiliar places now? You never used to be like that. You used to follow me around like a little puppy wherever I went."

I wasn't sure what point in time he was referring to. I certainly didn't remember ever doing such a thing, though it was certainly possible.

"What, did you forget all those times your mother asked us to run errands in the next town over? I'd always take you the most roundabout ways off the beaten path, but you never seemed to notice or care."

I did remember something along those lines. That was around the time Lord Crow had started playing tricks on me, and being a gullible little kid, I would take every word at face value. For decades, I kept using those paths, totally convinced they were shortcuts and not the exact opposite. Granted, it kept me in good shape, so I wasn't too mad about it, aside from being disappointed in myself for being so easily fooled. Thinking back on it, I should've realized a lot sooner that there was no need to cross over two mountains just to get into town. Our village wasn't *that* remote.

"That's different! I'm not the same person I was back then!" I cried.

"I certainly hope not," he teased.

His mocking tone ticked me off. Why was he incapable of having a normal conversation with me? "You really don't get it, do you?! God, why do you always have to treat me like such a kid?! And why do you still suck at even the most basic of small talk?!"

He really hadn't changed—it was almost like the man from my childhood was frozen in time. We beastfolk didn't show our ages, so at least it made sense that he looked the same.

"I still treat you like a kid because you *are* still a kid," he replied. "And I don't know what you mean by 'still.' I've never felt the need to partake in small talk—not now, not ever."

"Grr! I'm a grown woman, for your information! See, this is why you've been single your whole life! And you have such a handsome face too! Ugh, what a waste..."

Why did he seem so determined to remain alone? Wasn't it hard living by himself? Didn't he ever get sad or lonely? I could see how one who'd never known how good it feels to live along-side others might be able to get by without ever getting lonely, but I wasn't like that, and I didn't want that for Lord Crow. When everyone in the village died, and Lord Crow left me behind, it felt like there was a gaping hole in my heart. That was what being alone felt like—losing the ones you cared about most deeply. Sometimes, that gaping hole would ache all over again, suddenly and without warning. It was unbearable. It was suffocating. Admittedly, I lived in the palace surrounded by tons of people at all times now, so I didn't really get lonely anymore, but Lord Crow was different. And it didn't seem like he *wanted* to be alone. So why was he?

I asked him, and he simply gave me a self-deprecating grin. "I don't need anyone else...'cause I have no intention of ever being happy again."

"Wha..."

A single syllable fell out of my mouth as my eyes widened in horror.

"The moment I decided to dedicate my life to avenging my sister, I lost the ability to even think about my own happiness, and now I've even roped in an innocent kid to do my dirty work for me. Think it's pretty safe to say I'm going to hell."

I knew a little about his search for revenge—he'd told me about it back when we still lived in the village. How his dear little sister had been slain by one of our own during the Nightmare of Adorea calamity. He never told me who the perpetrator was, but whenever he talked about it, he got an intense look of rage and sorrow in his eyes. I'd forgotten an awful lot about my time with him back then, but that one image had stuck with me throughout the years.

But what did he mean about making an "innocent kid" do his dirty work? Was he planning to have someone else avenge her for him? Something told me Lord Crow wouldn't feel satisfied unless he got revenge himself. Besides, who could this "kid" even be? I had no clue. *Well, not like wondering's gonna get me anywhere. Maybe I should just come right out and ask.*

"Um, Lord Crow...?"

"What is it? We're here," he said, looking down at me without a hint of the pained expression he'd worn a moment ago. This startled me so much, I decided not to ask what I'd been planning and instead turned to see where he'd brought me.

"Whoa!"

It was like someone had rolled out the red carpet for us—the entire area was overgrown with deep red flowers I'd never seen before. Their vibrant crimson hue was almost foreboding, but they were beautiful nonetheless.

"We saw some of these growing along the road on the way here too. I didn't recognize them, but Akira sure did. Said there's a type of flower back in his world that looked exactly like 'em. They're called 'higanbana' or 'red spider lilies.'"

The flowers grew in massive clusters, their petals reaching up like long, thin fingers to the heavens. I reached out to touch one, but Lord Crow stopped me.

"They're poisonous, so I wouldn't recommend it. Maybe if we knew what part of the flower the poison was stored in, but Akira forgot. Not that I blame him. Hell, I was surprised a guy like him even knew the name of a flower."

"Really? How can something this beautiful be poisonous?"

As much as I wanted to pluck one, perhaps it would be a good idea to heed his warning and enjoy them from afar. They were more beautiful in large groups like this than alone in a vase anyhow.

"The 'higan' in higanbana apparently refers to a place called nirvana—their name for the place we go after death. You could say they're the flowers of the afterlife. Though even Akira didn't know exactly why they were named that."

"Nirvana, huh... They're so beautiful, though. Why associate them with death?"

Was there really no better name? What an unfortunate flower—first it was unlucky enough to be poisonous, then it got a morbid name. I couldn't help but feel bad for the poor flowers as I watched them sway in the wind.

"Well, they are pretty nice-looking, at least," said Lord Crow.

"Yeah. Why did you bring me here?"

I turned to look up at Lord Crow as he stared at the flowers.

He furrowed his brow and inclined his head as though he felt a little awkward. "Why? I was just walking around town yesterday and happened upon these, and I felt like showing them to someone... That's the only reason. No ulterior motives."

This did not seem like the sort of thing he would do purely by chance at all. To be fair, he had liked pretty flowers for as long as I'd known him. Those light-pink flowers that floated on lakes, those purple flowers whose petals fell from the sky like rain... He would always find places with flowers like that, then show them to me and me alone. I was sure I'd never forget the sight for the rest of my life. After living in the palace for so long, I'd almost forgotten just how beautiful flowers could be.

"You probably won't be able to memorize the way to get here, though, so don't try to come back here on your own," said Lord Crow, worried despite his tough façade.

"Then I guess I'll just have to drag you into coming along, won't I? Looks like we just added yet another secret spot to our repertoire," I joked.

"Wow, you actually remember those old trips?" Crow responded, gazing down at the red spider lilies with the slightest, almost imperceptible hint of a smile.

POV: ODA AKIRA

"PLEASE, you have to let me be your apprentice!"

"Absolutely not."

The lionman pleaded with twinkling eyes and a tail wagging fast enough to serve as a boat rudder. He looked like a puppy begging for a treat. How had I gotten myself into this situation? One minute he was on the floor begging for my forgiveness, and now he was imploring me to take him on as my pupil.

"Why not?!"

"Because I don't take apprentices, I don't have the skills to teach someone, and I don't know the first thing about you."

With this, Kerria swooped in to speak on Raúl's behalf. What was with these people? I would have appreciated it if Amelia would stop laughing and help me out of this pickle. And I was going to give Night (who was still struggling to suppress his own laughter) a piece of my mind when we got back to our hotel room.

After the lionman had first fallen to his knees before me, the rest of the adventurers still in the Guild had left (probably in fear of Amelia), and we'd sat down in their empty seats. I had hoped to leave right after them, as we had no business at the Guild and I didn't want to run into Gram, but before we made it to the door, Raúl, Kerria, and the shifty-eyed Mamoru blocked our path and forcibly treated us to tea by way of apology. Only, instead of tea cakes, we were treated to stories about Raúl and Kerria. I'd been certain they were lovers, but they were actually just childhood friends.

"Raúl and I have been inseparable ever since we were born. As you can see, my legs don't work, so he's been helping with the heavy lifting my whole life. He's also a huge worrywart, so he always hangs out at the Guild with me whenever he doesn't have any business to take care of."

"Bwuh?! I don't come here for *you*! It's my duty as a silver-rank adventurer to be here on call!"

"Yeah, yeah. So he says, while also being single-handedly responsible for stopping any and all bar fights and scaring any adventurer who says a single bad thing about me out of town."

"That's just a coincidence! Honest!"

The two of them began bickering again despite having been warned about it by the assistant guildmaster. They were obviously very close, so much so that I couldn't have been the only one to mistake them for a couple. Kerria had been born without the ability to walk, and after her parents died when she was young, Raúl stepped in. Maybe it was my own prejudices talking, but he didn't strike me as the type to go out of his way to help others. If anything, he seemed like the type to always need motherly guidance.

"Raúl's a pretty good cook too—better than your average chef, I'd say. And he does all the chores and everything. Bet you didn't expect that, huh?" Kerria told Amelia, almost as if she was bragging.

"No, I can't say I did. Wouldn't have expected that at all. Not. At. All," Amelia replied.

"All right, that's enough! You don't have to be so *rude* about it!" growled the lion in question, and Kerria went pale, apparently worried about how Amelia would take the outburst.

Over the course of our discussion, Raúl's internal hierarchy had become clear: I was the strongest person out there, followed by gold-rank adventurers, then himself and all the other silver-rank adventurers, then below *that* was where Amelia and everyone else fit in. Which struck me as kind of funny, given that Amelia was a silver-rank adventurer just like him. I wondered what his metrics were. Was it just because Amelia didn't *look* particularly strong? Because if anything, an argument could be made that she was stronger than *me*, considering she had a limitless supply of mana and a far greater depth of experience in battle and in this world. I had waltzed into this world not long ago and wasn't even using my skills the way they were intended. But

Amelia didn't seem too offended by Raúl's remarks, so I didn't make a big deal out of it.

"Cooking, huh? What's your specialty?" I asked.

"Well, uh... I can make a pretty mean stew out of general boar meat and potatoes. Sometimes I'll throw in a few carrots for good measure," he replied, scratching his cheek in embarrassment.

The difference between the way he talked to me and the way he talked to Amelia was night and day. I found myself wondering if the dish he described would taste anything like Japanese-style stewed meat and potatoes. At my house, we always threw carrots into the stew too, not to mention konjac, burdock, and taro. And general boar wasn't exactly the hardest monster to hunt either—any half-decent adventurer could take one down without too much trouble. They were stupid creatures that charged head-first into you, so as long as you knew when to dodge out of the way, you were all set. Their meat was pretty tasty when grilled or roasted, though it was too close to beef for my tastes. There were also regular boars here that were a fair bit smaller than general boars, but they weren't really good for meat and were instead hunted for their thick hides, which could fetch a decent price.

"So, whaddya say? If you agree to take Raúl on as your apprentice, you could come stay at our place and enjoy the high life with us!"

"Aha! I *knew* you were trying to wingman for me!"

And here I thought we'd changed the subject. This redheaded lion and his golden-haired cohort didn't know how to take no for an answer.

"Sorry, but we're on a bit of a journey, and we've got places to be. I can't afford to stay in any one place for too long," I told them.

"A journey, eh? And where is it you might be heading?"

Generally, an adventurer, despite the name, stuck to one or two towns, taking on requests from the local Guild branches. Guilds liked having strong and high-ranking adventurers on hand whenever a problem arose, so they tried to encourage people to settle in one place. However, I wasn't an ordinary adventurer, and I wouldn't have even registered with the Guild if it hadn't been a requirement for entering the Great Labyrinth of Brute. I also had no intention of settling down in this world or having someplace to call "home." My only home was back in my world with my mom and Yui, and as I'd already explained to Amelia and Night, nothing was going to change that.

"Let's just say that if I told you where we're headed, you'd probably laugh at me. That's the kind of place our final destination is," I said, attempting to gloss over things. Unless there was someone in this building who was itching for a war between the humans and beastfolk, I couldn't just go running my mouth about this sort of thing. Not that I expected anyone to believe me even if I *did* lay it all out on the table. That yes, I was summoned here via the hero summoning ritual, but no, I didn't really care about killing the Demon Lord. Surely this idiot who had taken it upon himself to develop vast delusions about me wouldn't be able to wrap his head around my circumstances.

"Somewhere we'd laugh at you for trying to go, eh? Any ideas, Kerria?"

"Nope, I got nothin'."

As the two of them attempted to puzzle it out, I downed the last of my tea and stood up. "I think it's about time we joined back up with our friends. Raúl and Kerria, it was nice to meet you."

We needed to find Crow and Lia, who'd probably lost track of time. Our hosts looked sad to see us leave, but their expressions brightened a bit when I said we'd still be in town for a few days. Now even Kerria was making the puppy-dog eyes at me.

"The tea was delicious, thank you," said Amelia, rising from her seat as well.

"Could you wait just one moment, please?" said an unfamiliar voice from the inner part of the building, just as I placed my hand on the doorknob.

It wasn't Mamoru or any of the other Guild employees. Amelia and I both turned to see a slightly chubby man standing at the opposite end of the room. He hadn't come in through the front door, so he was Guild personnel...but his presence was rather ominous. That impression wasn't helped as the other Guild workers' faces turned grim the moment he appeared. Or the fact that he was blatantly undressing Amelia with his eyes.

"Miss Amelia Rosequartz, I take it?" the man asked with a devious grin. "Gram Cluster, owner and operator of the Uruk Adventurer's Guild. There's something I'd like to discuss with you in private. Would you be a dear and come speak with me in my office?"

I scowled. Here he was—Gram, in the flesh. The man who led demons into the Great Labyrinth of Brute so they could kidnap

Amelia, who wanted to chop her up and sell her organs on the black market for winning the pageant, and who had killed Crow's little sister. None of his attempts at Amelia had been successful, but there was no denying they'd caused us a serious amount of harm. Normally, this would be when I grabbed him by the collar and gave him a piece of my mind, but that didn't seem to be a good idea. We needed an exit strategy; it would be nice to make it out of here without any trouble.

I could hear his greasy face smacking around as he spoke, but I was vehemently opposed to acknowledging this asshole's existence, so I didn't even deign to look his way. I stepped in front of Amelia to protect her from having to look at him and to keep his eyes off her.

"Oh? And who might you be? I was having a conversation with Miss Amelia, if you don't mind," said Gram.

Now his eyes were locked right on me. I got goosebumps; it was extremely rare for me to hate another person as much as I hated Gram. I'd never even hated any of my unintelligible or obnoxiously temperamental teachers this much.

When I refused to respond, Gram took a real look at me for the first time and, noticing my outfit, clapped his hands. "Oh, I see. You're Miss Amelia's escort, are you? Well, good work, sir. I will take her from here. Return to your homeland and rest easy."

What was this guy going on about? I *was* kind of like her bodyguard, but I wasn't gonna let the rest of that crap fly. He was speaking as if I'd fulfilled my duties and it was time to hand over the girl.

"Beg your pardon?" I said in a threatening voice so low that it even took me by surprise. Nearby, I could see Raúl and Kerria trembling in fright. Apparently, my malice was plain to see for all but Gram.

"What, have you not been paid yet? How much did the elven king offer you? I'll pay you double that, so consider yourself relieved from duty. How did a lowly human like you even manage to get so close to Miss Amelia in the first place? Did you seduce her?"

This guy had a fairly low opinion of humans. There was nothing worse than a guy who truly believed all of the awful crap that came out of his mouth, and Raúl wasn't about to sit back and listen to him insult me.

"Watch your mouth. That's the Silent Assassin you're talking to, not to mention a summoned hero. You might be the guildmaster here, but I won't stand by and let you disrespect him like that," he said, puffing out his chest as he stepped forward in my defense. I really wished he hadn't done that.

Immediately, the look in Gram's eyes changed. "So you're a summoned hero, are you? Well, that's awfully strange."

"How so?" I asked, despite my better judgment.

"From what I've heard, the current party of summoned heroes has only ever left Retice Castle once, to do a trial run down in the Great Labyrinth of Kantinen, and they've been sequestered in the castle ever since. So how could the summoned hero himself be here right now? Finally felt like getting off your rear end and slaying the Demon Lord, did you?"

All of the previous heroes had contributed something to the development of this world. Some may not have slain the Demon Lord, but all of them at least did something to make the lives of its people better. Things like cameras, for example, which didn't seem like they belonged in this world, had been introduced by heroes. But our party of heroes hadn't really accomplished anything since being summoned here, with most of my classmates refusing to fight and remaining cooped up in the castle. Most people probably thought we were no-good, lazy deadbeats—and they were probably right. All we'd done in our time here, as far as they knew, was learn how to fight and take a trip to a labyrinth, but the truth was that the average citizen had no idea how unreasonable their expectations of the summoned heroes were. We'd been summoned here from a world at peace, most of us never having even been in a fistfight before, yet they thought that as heroes, we owed it to them to do *something* to improve their lives, not realizing how selfish that mindset was or that we hadn't come here by choice.

"I may have come here via the hero summoning ritual, but I'm not your hero. And we have no intention of slaying the Demon Lord," I said at last.

"I see, so you're not *the* hero. But what's this nonsense about not wanting to slay the Demon Lord? That is the job of a summoned hero and his party. That is your purpose in this world, and that is how it has always been."

Why did the people of this world always try to foist their problems onto someone else? If they were genuinely in dire straits and got on their knees begging for our assistance, that would be one thing, but from what I could tell, the king of Retice had no intention of ever trying to help us slay the Demon Lord. Unfortunately for him, we weren't simply puppets who took orders and carried them out without question. We had our own emotions and misgivings about killing other people without any real justification. And so he'd used his daughter to try to place a curse on us all. I still remembered the curse I overheard her placing over the main hero: "May the hero ever embody his title, both in words and in deeds..." In other words, they just wanted us to be the idealized heroes the people of this world expected us to be. And I wasn't here for that.

"I don't give a damn what you think my 'purpose' here is. We were dragged here against our will from a world where people actually know how to get along for the most part. How 'bout you guys try solving your own problems for a change? Don't expect people from another world to always be there to do your dirty work."

I had no intention of being a good Samaritan like the summoned heroes of old. Maybe my classmates would, through no will of their own, be the heroes everyone wanted them to be since they were still under the curse, but I wasn't the type to do something purely out of the goodness of my heart. I didn't work without compensation unless it was something I genuinely wanted to do. I didn't take orders from anyone.

Gram raised an eyebrow, then brought his face close to mine. I took a single step back as he whispered quietly to me so no one else would hear. "Then I take it you have no intention of grant-ing the dying wish of the foolish oaf who sacrificed himself just so you could escape the castle? Would you like to know what his last words were? I could tell you. He mentioned an 'Akira'— that's your name, I take it?" he asked, and my blood began to boil. "Oh, his final moments were so entertaining to watch, let me tell you. I'm so glad I decided to equip the Night Ravens with body cameras."

"So you *did* murder Commander Saran…"

I hadn't been there for the commander's final moments. Obviously, I wanted to know what his last words were, but more than anything, I was just glad to finally know for certain who had killed him.

"Well, do you want to know or not? If you'd just come along with Miss Amelia, I'd be happy to tell you all about it."

But I simply laughed and shook my head. "You just made a huge mistake in telling me that, my friend." This time, it was me who put my face close to his. "If I were you, I'd sleep with one eye open tonight."

Finally, I'd found him. The man I was meant to kill. The one I had to assassinate.

"Oh, I'm sorry you feel that way," said Gram, "but I'm afraid you won't be leaving here alive."

The moment Gram finished speaking, he snapped his fingers, and three men garbed in all black appeared as if from nowhere. Their eyes were lifeless, and I knew immediately they were under the influence of Gram's boosters. The only other people left in the

Guild building aside from me and Amelia were Night, Raúl, and Kerria; Mamoru and the other employees had long since fled the scene. That was fine by me, since it meant I could fight without worrying about accidental casualties. But just as I was starting to plan out my first move, Kerria wheeled herself forward until she was sitting right in front of Gram.

"Guildmaster, what is the meaning of this?! This man is an adventurer! You can't just—"

Gram cut her off. "How impudent for a commoner like you— and a human, no less—to address a member of the royal family such as I. Kill her along with the other human cur. It's time for me to collect what is rightfully mine."

With that, one of the men in black sent Kerria flying across the room, wheelchair and all. Her head hit the wall with a loud crack, and she fell to the floor in a heap. Blood poured from her forehead; if she didn't receive treatment, and fast, she might die. All the man had done was take a single swing at her with his fist, and it was enough to send her careening into the wall. These drugged-up mercenaries were not to be underestimated.

"Kerria! You *bastard*!" screamed Raúl as he lunged at the mercenary responsible.

I could only watch out of the corner of my eye, since I had the other two mercenaries to worry about, but I could immediately see why he was called "Raúl the Whirlwind." His movements were fast and tempestuous, without even a moment's hesitation.

"You take care of Kerria while I deal with these guys!" I yelled, catching one of their fists and grasping it tightly in my hand.

"You got it!" he cried back.

"Get down on the ground!" shouted Amelia as I wrapped my other arm around her. With her Gravity Magic, she wouldn't have too much trouble taking care of the other two mercenaries, but I was worried about Raúl, who was slowed down by the fact that he was carrying Kerria's unconscious body under one arm.

"Night! We can handle these two—you go help Raúl! Just don't kill 'em."

"On it," said Night, hopping down from my shoulders. He used Shapeshifter to turn into the cheetah form he'd used down in the Great Labyrinth of Brute and raced over to Raúl's aid.

"That girl is my property, and you will return her to me right this instant!" demanded Gram, reaching out his hand as he walked over to us.

Something snapped inside me, and I slapped his hand away with a disgusted grimace. "Amelia doesn't belong to you! She's mine, so keep your grubby hands off her!" I screamed, tightening my grip on the mercenary's fist. "Shadow Magic, activate!"

Our shadows combined at our fists. I took control and sent them wriggling and writhing across the floor.

"Make an escape route for us, boys!" I commanded, and the shadows quickly gobbled up the heavy door blocking the entrance to the Adventurer's Guild. "Night, Amelia! Time to blow this joint!"

"Got it!"

"Right behind you!"

Amelia used her Gravity Magic to force Gram and the three men in black to their knees, as Night (still in cheetah form) sprinted over with Raúl and Kerria on his back before leaping out of the gaping hole where the door had once stood.

"Damn you! Don't let them escape! What are you three doing?! Get up, you imbeciles! Hurry up and go after them!"

With Gram screaming at us to no avail, Amelia and I took our leave of the Adventurer's Guild. I was expecting to be surrounded again once we made it outside, but there were no other men in black in sight. The only people around were a few adventurers and rubberneckers who'd heard the commotion and had come to see what was up. Night was long gone, and since I didn't remember how we'd gotten here, I had no clue which way to go.

"Hey, Mister! Up here!"

Recognizing Latticenail's voice, I looked up to find she was flying through the sky, holding on to what looked like a giant white wing. She swooped down and reached out a hand down to pick us up.

"Amelia!" I yelled.

"Ready!" she replied.

Clasping Amelia's hand tightly in mine, I kicked off the ground and grabbed hold of Latticenail's hand, and the two of us were pulled up into the sky.

"Man, flying sure is fun, don'tcha think?" said Latticenail, who wasn't struggling at all to support the extra weight. "Good thing those doped-up mercenaries can't fly too, am I right?"

"Thanks, Latticenail. You really helped us out of a bind there," I said, noticing the cuts and scrapes all across her body. I assumed Gram had had the entire building surrounded, and she had picked up on this before we'd even set foot into the Guild. Hence why she had opted to remain outside—it seemed she'd taken care of all of them single-handedly.

"Nah, don't mention it! I like you guys, and I'd feel awful if you were to die on my watch!" she said proudly. She really had saved our bacon. If we'd tried to escape on foot, they probably would have caught up to us sooner or later.

We rose higher and higher into the sky until we could see the entirety of Uruk spread out below us.

"It's so pretty..." Amelia breathed.

Boats were making their way gently down the canals, and all the people walking down the streets were reduced to the size of ants. The waters for which the city was known shimmered like precious gems.

"Yeah, it is," I whispered, not even knowing that at that very moment, in another corner of the city, Crow and Lia were looking straight up at us.

The Kill

POV: ODA AKIRA

AFTER NARROWLY ESCAPING the clutches of Gram and his henchmen, we regrouped at the hotel room. Apparently, Crow and Lia had seen us flying through the sky and decided to rush back to see what was up. I felt a little bad for having brought an abrupt end to their alone time—Lia gave me a bit of flak for it, but as soon as I told her about our run-in with Gram, she graciously let me off the hook.

Latticenail had gone waltzing off somewhere before I even noticed, but the good news was that, despite her grievous wounds, it looked like Kerria was going to make a full recovery. Though the doctor did say that if we hadn't taken her in when we did, it might have been too late. She and Raúl made it sound like they were going to quit the Adventurer's Guild and go live in another town entirely...which was understandable, given what had just happened between them and the guildmaster.

And so it was that I found myself awake in the hotel room in the middle of the night, while everyone else was fast asleep. It must have been between two and three in the morning—the true dead of night. I slowly got out of bed, taking care so as not to wake Amelia or Night beside me. I donned my great black cloak, which I didn't often wear since it only got in the way, and wrapped my black scarf around my neck. My usual garb was already pitch-black, but now I was as dark as the night itself and could move completely undetected. As luck would have it, tonight was a new moon. Thanks to my Assassination ability, I had excellent night vision, which would help me avoid detection.

"You headed out?" asked Crow, who'd woken up and was now standing in the doorway.

"Yeah," I replied. I was expecting him to see me off, so I wasn't surprised.

"I know this probably rings hollow coming from the guy who put you up to this, but don't overdo it if things get sketchy. That demon girl said those drugged-up mercenaries are about as strong as the average demon."

I wasn't sure when he'd had a chance to talk to Latticenail, but I couldn't help but laugh at his warning. I wasn't about to be put off by the prospect of having to fight an ordinary demon, and Crow should have known as much. He was probably just getting a little anxious now that the hour was close at hand, and feeling bad for having put me in this position.

"This isn't like you, Crow. Don't worry, I would've ended up doing this eventually whether you asked me to or not. I swore to myself when I left the castle that I'd avenge Commander Saran even if it was the last thing I did, and now I finally have the chance to do just that. You can still feel free to wish me luck, though."

I equipped my twin daggers and walked right past Crow and out of the room. He followed.

"Y'know, the moment I first laid eyes on you at that inn back in Ur, I knew you were out to get revenge. I could see it in your eyes," he told me.

"I'll bet. No offense, but I always felt like focusing on nothing but revenge was an exhausting way to live. I worry that me getting vengeance for your sister isn't gonna make you feel at peace, or like justice has been served, or anything like that."

As I checked to make sure each and every throwing knife I had concealed on my body was secure, I heard Crow let out a derisive snort. Of course, he would know how exhausting it was to be angry—and how remaining angry over the same thing for years on end would take a massive toll on a person's stamina.

"Yeah, maybe not, but you'll at least be eliminating the source of a disease that's been plaguing beastfolk society and this entire world for far too long. He's always been the one pulling the strings and reaping the benefits. All of his underlings are merely being used."

I had often wondered why a man who supposedly didn't have any allies or underlings he could trust hadn't already been assassinated, and now I knew it was likely because of his drugged-up mercenaries. They were, after all, nothing more than lifeless puppets who only knew how to fight and follow orders. He didn't need to earn their trust, nor did he need to worry about them betraying him. After fighting some today, I was sure I'd be able to slip past them and murder Gram right under their noses.

With my Conceal Presence skill at Max Level, I could just waltz right in without even showing up on their security cameras. Hell, even if they had some sort of infrared sensors to detect body heat, my skill seemed to defy and distort the very laws of physics to make me literally imperceptible, so even those wouldn't be able to detect me. The only exception I'd come across was Commander Saran and his Mystic Eyes.

Growing up, I never liked that I could go completely unnoticed by others. Especially when I was a very little kid playing on the playground and ended up forgotten or left behind. That loneliness was crushing at times. Granted, it had its uses once I made it to high school, when I could skip class or sleep in the middle of a lecture without getting caught, but it wasn't as if I ever *liked* the ability—even after coming to this world where it was a tangible skill with practical applications. But right now, things were different. For the first time in my life, I could honestly say that I was grateful to have this power.

Gram had hurt so many people throughout his reign of terror. People like my friend and mentor, Commander Saran, and Crow's sister, and even my beloved Amelia. Just today, he'd almost killed Kerria for no good reason. And as long as he was allowed to remain alive, he'd only continue to hurt more innocent people.

"I'm not planning to kill any of his mercenaries, for the record. But if I run into any other assassins who are after the same target,

I'll have no choice but to eliminate them. Under no circumstances will I let anyone else steal this kill from us. I will only kill Gram and any other assassins who get in my way. Is that okay with you, oh, honorable client of mine?" I asked sarcastically.

"Yep, that works for me...oh, trusty assassin of mine."

As Crow looked at me with remorseful eyes, I flashed him a halfhearted smile, then jumped out the window.

"Wait, Akira! Don't do this!"

A fair princess called my name, but I pretended not to hear.

I knelt atop the slanted rooftop of the building Gram called home, my silhouette every bit as dark as the night sky behind me. I loomed there for quite a while—watching, waiting—utterly motionless aside from the fluttering of my cloak and long black scarf in the midnight breeze.

I needed to avoid fighting his mercenaries. I had done no preparations in advance, so I didn't know what times the guards made their rounds. With the help of Conceal Presence, it would be easy for me to slip in and kill Gram, but things could still turn out badly for me if they discovered he was dead before I could escape. It would have been better to draft up a more organized plan beforehand, but given there was a chance I might have changed my mind, or that Gram could have discovered where we were staying, I couldn't risk waiting any longer. Hence why I needed to scope the place out, watching carefully for the right moment.

I spent a good while monitoring the goings-on in and around the building. After some time, I rose to my feet with a sigh,

drew my twin Yato-no-Kami daggers, and readied for combat. A man emerged directly in front of me, seemingly out of thin air. Just like me, he was garbed all in black and lightly armored. Another assassin had arrived to get in my way, just as I had feared. Obviously, Gram had no shortage of enemies who might pay to see him offed, but I'd hoped could get through tonight without encountering any other assassins.

The only noticeable differences between myself and the man was that I had daggers and he had a sword, and that I had my black cloak and scarf. They really did get in the way of an assassin's work, so this didn't surprise me. I'd only taken these extra items from the castle because I thought they'd look cool, but it wasn't as though they had any practical use beyond some camouflage. I didn't find them cumbersome, but there was no denying that they were unnecessary.

The other man and I locked eyes, glaring at each other for a moment before the other man lost his nerve and looked away.

"Well, look who it is," the man said. "You here to guard the place, hotshot? Or are you just out to slit our poor guildmaster's throat?"

Apparently, I'd become quite famous among my fellow assassins, which struck me as kind of funny, given I'd yet to carry out a single assassination.

"And yours, if you try to get in my way," I responded matter-of-factly, making it clear that I had no intention of letting anyone stop me from doing what I came here to do. Unless this guy was even dumber than Raúl, surely he'd take the hint and stand down.

I had conveyed my vendetta, plain and simple, and I could see the other man shaking in his boots. He was much more of a rookie than I expected; I would have thought anyone who dared to try their hand at assassinating a man protected by an army of souped-up mercenaries would at least have the skills to get the job done.

"Well, that's just great. Never thought I'd get the chance to go toe-to-toe with the Silent Assassin himself. Lucky me," the man said, sighing in resignation.

He braced himself for combat, but I could tell his mind was flip-flopping between fight or flight. In his current state, it was clear that even if he swung that sword of his, it would have all the force of a wet paper towel behind it. The sheer malice I was exuding made him break out in a cold sweat. I simply stared at the wimpy man without a shred of empathy, like a hunter would stare down its prey. I waited until just before the man was about to exhale, then lunged forward with my dagger and tore through the frigid night air.

Before the man even knew what hit him, he fell to the ground with his eyes wide in horror and his hands clutching at his neck, trying to stop the geyser of blood now spurting from his throat. Only a moment later, he choked out his final breath and lay still on the cold rooftop. I stood up straight, wiping the blood off of my dagger.

It was the first time I'd ever killed another human being, yet I didn't feel strongly about it. I wasn't sure if that was the result of my Assassination skill trying to mitigate the shock, or if I was simply that cold and unfeeling, but I let out a sigh of relief nonetheless; I'd been worried actually killing another man might make me lose my nerve.

Meanwhile, it seemed the night watchmen inside had thinned out. Thankfully, they hadn't noticed the duel that had just taken place outside. Perhaps these zombified mercenaries were also incredibly dense or unobservant.

Activating Conceal Presence first, I used my Assassination skill to unlock a nearby window and slip into the bedchambers of my true quarry for the evening. I looked down at Gram as he lay there, snoring loudly.

My dagger quivered slightly in my trembling hand as I held it aloft, despite the fact that I'd just easily killed someone. I brought my other hand up to hold the blade steady, then tiptoed quietly across the room to press it against Gram's neck. To think that as soon as this blade hit its mark, I'd be saying goodbye to any chance of ever returning to the peaceful life I once enjoyed.

"Sorry, guys, but I have to do this. It's the only way I'll ever find closure. With this one man's death, I'll be exacting justice for so many people. And one in particular..."

I whispered these words of reassurance to my mother and Yui as a specter of the boy I had been—a typical high schooler by the name of Oda Akira—then mustered my strength and made a single, decisive slash.

After only a few short convulsions, Gram breathed his last. A shame he hadn't suffered longer, considering all the long years Crow and so many others had suffered. This wretched villain had caused so much so many different people so much pain over the course of his pathetic life, yet in the end, he only had to endure for a single second.

I didn't regret killing him, nor did I feel any sense of satisfaction for having successfully carried out my revenge. The only thing I felt was a deep and singular emptiness—one that ate at me like a gaping hole in my chest.

AFTERWORD

THANK YOU SO MUCH for purchasing this, the third volume of the *Assassin* series, for your reading pleasure. It's been a decent while since the release of Volume Two, hasn't it? As you probably noticed, this volume's epilogue was the very same scene that was foreshadowed in the prologue to Volume One, which means we've finally come full circle! But this doesn't mean Akira's story is over. Rest assured that our hero's adventures with his merry band of misfits will continue in future volumes.

Recently, I started working part-time at a bakery not too far from where I live, and I have to say, it's surprisingly backbreaking work! Combine this with the constant influx of customers eager to buy up pastries for the Christmas season, and I've developed a newfound respect for bakers and pâtissiers the world over. I know things will probably ease up once the new year rolls around, but I honestly can't believe just how busy it's gotten. If you're ever in the area and just so happen to stop by, I wholeheartedly recommend our strawberry tart.

I suppose that's about it from me, though I would like to take this opportunity to mention that the first volume of the *Assassin* manga adaptation should be releasing under the COMIC GARDO label right alongside this third volume of the novel. Hiroyuki Aigamo has done a spectacular job of bringing my story to life in manga format, so I really urge you to check it out. Speaking of artists, thank you once again to Tozai for drawing the lovely illustrations for this volume. I would also like to thank my editor and proofreader for their help in making this book possible. I do hope you'll look forward to what the future of the *Assassin* franchise has in store.